MW01196710

EDMOND HAMILTON'S
CAPTAIN FUTURE

The Guns of Pluto

(The Return of Ul Quorn, Book II)

by
Allen Steele

Copyright © 2019, 2020 by Coyote Steele LLC.

Newton's Laws of Thrills © 2020 by Paul Di Filippo.

Cover art © 2020 by Renan Boe.

Interior art © 2020 by M.D. Jackson.

Comet II illustration © 2019 by Rob Caswell.

Amazing Stories, *Amazing Selects* and their logos are wholly owned
trademarks of Experimenter Publishing Company, LLC.

"The Guns of Pluto" is an original *Amazing Selects publication.*

"The Harpers of Titan" originally appeared in *Startling Stories*,
September 1950. Permission to publish this story granted by
arrangement with Spectrum Literary Agency.

Captain Future, along with all characters and situations associated
with the original Captain Future created by Edmond Hamilton, are
used by kind permission of the Spectrum Literary Agency,
representing the literary estate of Edmond Hamilton, and the
Huntington National Bank.

Contents

Introduction:
Newton's Laws of Thrills
by Paul Di Filippo

When I reviewed the first of Haffner Press' wonderful Edmond Hamilton reissues in 2009 for Scott Edelman's *Sci-Fi Wire*, I could not foresee that offstage a vast and powerful intelligence was secretly conspiring to breathe new life into one of Hamilton's greatest creations, Captain Future. I innocently believed that fans of the Captain would have to content themselves merely with smart new editions of his classic adventures, resigning themselves to vintage thrills which, while still potent, would never reflect the realities of twenty-first century science fiction. So, never daring to hope for more, I simply praised Hamilton's work as "timeless and immortal storytelling...that still delivers pure entertainment," and urged readers young and old to seek him out.

(You'll be able to judge if my characterization of the original Captain Future tales was correct when you read the newly reprinted novella "The Harpers of Titan," which our valiant and perspicacious publisher is bringing to you along with the volume you now hold. But more on that in a minute.)

Imagine my surprise some eight years later, in 2017, when the identity and plans of that secret admirer and revivalist burst into the public spotlight with the appearance of *Avengers of the Moon*, a fully authorized relaunch and re-envisioning of the Captain Future mythos.

Who was that lone hero who had made such an unexpected treat possible? None other than my friend, Allen Steele, famed for his illustrious string of novels set in his own personal playgrounds. What a sly dog.

When I got a chance to review *Avengers of the Moon* – this time for *Locus Online* – I was thrilled to find that Allen had done the franchise full justice. Allow me to quote myself a bit:

The Captain's retro yet timeless virtues – both the hero's personal creed and the narrative stylings – are arguably congruent with cultural trends today toward a desired and desirable return to basics and old verities with a useful revisioning. And this type of space opera is essentially an infinite canvas on which new adventures can be perpetually inscribed.

As for the choice of author to pick up the Captain's tale – well, who else on the current scene might one nominate? It would have to be, I think, someone of a certain age. It's not likely a Millennial writer would care for the job or bring the appropriate zest and fondness to the task. So that limits our choices. Mike Resnick or Stephen Baxter or Robert Sawyer or David Brin or Catherine Asaro or C. J. Cherryh would do a fine job. But not necessarily better than Steele's loving performance. As he says in his "Afterword," his novel is "neither an homage to the Hamilton novels nor a parody, but rather an effort to bring Captain Future into the twenty-first century for a new generation of readers."

I think Steele has succeeded wonderfully, while still retaining all the old virtues and attractions of the original property.

Emerging from this unexpected reunion with Captain Future, I fully expected to have Curt Newton's suspenseful and fun adventures showing up in my TBR pile at regular intervals. But as with all archetypal odysseys, there was trouble ahead. As Steele explained in the afterword to "Captain Future in Love:"

I originally intended for *Avengers of the Moon* to be the first volume of a trilogy, to be followed by *The Guns of Pluto* and *The Horror at Jupiter* (the last an homage to the original title of the first

Captain Future novel). Unfortunately, very shortly after I turned in the final revisions of *Avengers of the Moon* to David Hartwell, my editor at Tor, David died in a tragic household accident. The young editor who succeeded David was less enamored with Captain Future than he had been; indeed, before she was given *Avengers of the Moon* to line-edit, she had no idea who the character was or his place in SF's history. I'm not sure she even liked space opera, or at least not the variety I'm writing. So, she killed the next two books, despite the fact that *Avengers* had favorable reviews, positive reader response, and solid sales in all its editions. No other publisher was interested in continuing a trilogy whose first volume was published by someone else.

But thanks to the good taste and boldness of *Amazing Stories* and its crew, this barrier was overcome, and now we have fresh adventures of Captain Future once more in our laps, so to speak. And his appearance in quasi-serial format – the installment before this one was *Captain Future in Love (The Return of Ul Quorn, Book I)* – befits the old-school ambiance even better perhaps than seeing him in fancy hardcover dress.

The installment which I just named picked up the story hard on the heels of *Avengers*. Curt and his posse – Otho, Grag and Simon, together dubbed the Futuremen – are now authorized and sanctioned secret guardians of the Solar Coalition civilization – although the honor chafes somewhat on the still young and rebellious Curt. So while assigned to a case, he runs away in a fit of self-indulgence – our hero is no brass saint – and takes up with a charming female criminal named Ashi Lanyr. Eventually forced to give up his unrealistic dreams of no responsibilities as a rogue, Curt is reunited with the Futuremen and Ashi disappears. We jump ahead some years however, and the woman resurfaces, still addicted to her criminal ways. Captain Future takes pity on her and installs her on his ship – where we learn, *sotto voce*, that she intends something malign. Signal the title card that says "Stay tuned!"

The Guns of Pluto (The Return of Ul Quorn, Book II) does not immediately take us back aboard the *Comet II*, but instead shows us some sizzling action on Pluto, the location of a max-security prison. Steele describes the forbidding environment with panache and zest, making the reader feel the alienness. Then appears the pleasure ship that was hijacked in the earlier volume, now seemingly in distress. But of course, we know that the ship is still manned by the mysterious Black Pirate and his henchmen. Soon, the Black Pirate has his way with the prison facility and warders, and Captain Future finds his fate commingled with that of the Plutonians. Coming along with the regular crew are IPF enforcer Joan Randall, inamorata of Curt, and her crusty boss Ezra Gurney. Together, they are going to encounter High Fiendishness in Bizarre Places: Allen Steele has a huge number of clever reversals, reveals and riots up his sleeve. I think this installment, really a short novel on its own, might pack in more heart-bumping incidents, world-building and character deepening than either *Avengers* or *In Love*. The lucky reader is in for an extremely rewarding and satisfying ride – except for that moment when he or she turns the last page and is faced with Steele's diabolical cliffhanger! Then the cursing will begin!

The dialogue scintillates, the villains crackle, and the good guys evoke respect, love and concern. As well, the pure science-fictional aspects of the novella provide the same sterling sense of wonder for which originator Edmond Hamilton was famous. Allen Steele has a lock now on this mode of resurgent classic space opera, and I have no doubt that installments three and four of this tale will provide as many Newtonian frissons, if not more.

And harking back to the One and Onlie Begettor, Hamilton, we should give up some admiration for his classic pulp prowess, as exhibited in "The Harpers of Titan." In just under ten thousand words, Hamilton conjures up an eerie ecology and an otherwordly culture with a long backstory. Then, by focusing on the plight of Simon the Brain, who must forego his serene cyborg existence to reanimate in the flesh, Hamilton plunges us into an epistemological quandary worthy of Plato. Finally, with his invention of the alien Harpers, he gives us a creepy menace that might have come from Clark Ashton Smith.

The visionary fire of science fiction that once filled Hamilton's veins now flows in a worthy heir!

Publisher's Introduction

D ive right in.

You don't really need an introduction to inform you that you are about to read something special. There's a good chance you already know this. I'm pretty confident of that assumption because we've given you four good reasons to assume specialness right on the cover.

There is a good reason why the names and words "Amazing Stories," "Amazing Selects," "Allen Steele," and "Captain Future," appear on that cover, not the least of which is the fact that this novella is a story about Captain Future written by none other than the award-winning author Allen Steele.

Those two facts alone ought to be enough to encourage you to plunk your quarter down for a chance to see the Egress. If you are still a bit hesitant, please allow this carnival barker a few more words.

One name I didn't mention was Edmond Hamilton. That name is on the cover too; if the name Allen Steele isn't enough for you to immediately ignore me and start turning pages, well, Edmond "Star Wrecker" Hamilton ought to be.

You see, Edmond was one of the earliest, if not the first, guy to realize that if you are playing around with faster than light travel, galaxy-spanning empires, and time-spanning millennia, your fleets are going to number in the tens of thousands of ships, your ships are going to be planet-sized, and your weapons are going to be capable of destroying entire star systems at one go.

Edmond, who died the same year that "Star Wars" was introduced to world-wide audiences, would have found the Death Star amusing. After all, he'd been writing about "galaxies far, far away" for fifty years by then. If asked about the movie, I'm pretty sure he'd have said something like, "Let me know when they come up with something original."

Which brings us back around to Captain Future. Edmond Hamilton created the Captain during the height of the pulp magazines, 1939 to be exact. Folks wanted heroes back then, and science fiction readers wanted science fiction heroes, and boy, did Edmond deliver. Some of the greatest names in the genre contributed epic stories to the *Captain Future Magazine*, Ray Bradbury, Henry Kuttner and Jack Williamson among them.

Still haven't turned the page? Well then, know this: Allen Steele has been known to write some great SF himself, and one of the things that inspired him to do so was Edmond Hamilton's Captain Future. Revamping and updating the Captain has been a dream and goal of Allen's for years.

Which means that what you are about to read is great science fiction; written by a great science fiction author, inspired by great science fiction; written by another great science fiction author!

Wait! I've not yet told you about the other two good reasons for reading this novella which appear on the cover: "*Amazing Stories*" and "*Amazing Selects*." The world's first science fiction magazine is going to be bringing you carefully selected, novella-length works under the *Amazing Selects* banner. "The Guns of Plato" is the second of what we hope will be a series of great reads: modern stories with a pulp feel. The first, "Captain Future in Love," was published 11/2019 and can be purchased in either electronic or paper format.

– Steve Davidson

Publisher

Who Is Captain Future?

Captain Future is the *nom de guerre* of Curt Newton, adventurer, citizen-scientist, and troubleshooter for the Interplanetary Police Force (IPF) of the Solar Coalition. Although born on Earth, Curt was raised on the Moon, his very existence a closely-guarded secret following the murder of his parents, Roger and Elaine Newton, within their underground laboratory hidden beneath the floor of Tycho Crater.

Roger and Elaine, along with their teacher and mentor Simon Wright, were visionary scientists working on the development of a prototype android which they named Otho (an acronym for "Orthogenetic Transhuman Organism") that was intended to be a full-body replacement for the terminally ill Dr. Wright. It was their hope that, if Dr. Wright's mind could be successfully scanned into Otho's brain, he would be the first of many people who'd have their lives expanded indefinitely by such transfers.

However, shortly before Roger, Elaine, and Simon were about to enter the final phases of this project, they learned that their principal financial investor, Victor Corvo, had other plans for the new technology: selling it to the military to supply soldiers killed in combat with new bodies, in the process creating immortal armies. Seeing this as both unethical and dangerous, the three scientists decided to take the newborn Curt and flee to the Moon, where they'd finish Otho's development at remote Tycho Base, which Roger secretly built beneath the lunar surface with the aid of construction robots. In order to keep Corvo from learning where they'd gone, Roger Newton faked their death aboard his private racing yacht.

Upon arrival at Tycho Base, though, Simon Wright succumbed to the stress of the voyage from Earth. Fortunately, Roger and Elaine were able to preserve his brain and transfer it into a robotic, multi-functional drone. They also realized that one of the construction robots used to build the base had become a sentient and intelligent being who had taken the name of the company that manufactured him, Grag, as his own. Because it's useful to have an intelligent robot, Roger and Elaine decided to keep Grag while Simon learned to use the drone that his brain temporarily would occupy until Otho's body had finished its development within the experimental bioclast that Roger and Elaine had fashioned for the purpose.

Before this could happen, though, tragedy – and homicide – struck. Several months after the family's arrival on the Moon, Tycho Base had an unexpected visitor: Victor Corvo. Upon figuring out that Roger Newton faked the deaths of himself and his party, Corvo tracked them to Luna. And he didn't come alone, but instead brought with him a pair of killers-for-hire. During the confrontation that followed, Corvo had his assassins murder Roger and Elaine. However, Simon Wright witnessed the double-murder from his hiding place in Tycho's subsurface lair, where Roger had told him to take Curt when Corvo's ship landed. Simon ordered Grag to kill the assassins; however, Corvo managed to get away, leaving behind a bomb that devastated Tycho Base's above ground facilities, but didn't impact the hidden warrens below.

Having assumed that Roger Newton and his family were dead, Corvo fled back to Earth, unwittingly leaving behind Simon Wright, Curt Newton, Grag and the soon-to-be-born Otho. Vowing to avenge the murders of Roger and Elaine, Simon took it upon himself to raise Curt in secrecy, training him for the day when he could track down Victor Corvo.

With Simon, Grag and Otho as both his teachers and companions, Curt Newton spent the first decades of his life learning the skills he'd need for this task. In doing so Simon Wright – whom

Otho and Curt nicknamed "the Brain" – gave Curt an appellation of his own: Captain Future, after the make-believe persona Curt fashioned for himself while playing in Tycho's underground passageways. The grown-up Curt was reluctant to use this childhood nickname, but the Brain insisted that he needed to keep his true identity a carefully-guarded secret as he pursued his campaign against Corvo, who, since his murder of Curt's parents, had become an elected member of the Solar Coalition Senate.

Eventually, Corvo was brought to justice. In doing so, Curt exposed a plot to destroy the Solar Coalition that Corvo had hatched along with his illegitimate son: Ul Quorn, the so-called Magician of Mars, who was the leader of the Starry Messenger separatist movement. Curt refused to kill Senator Corvo, though, instead turning him over to the IPF. Once this was done, James Carthew – the President of the Solar Alliance whom Corvo had targeted for assassination – persuaded Curt to continue his newfound role as the Solar Coalition's troubleshooter.

Along with Lieutenant Joan Randall of the IPF (with whom Curt is not-so-secretly infatuated) and Simon, Otho and Grag as his companions, Captain Future and the Futuremen – the name given by President Carthew to Curt's friends, teachers and companions – became the protectors of law and justice on the high frontier.

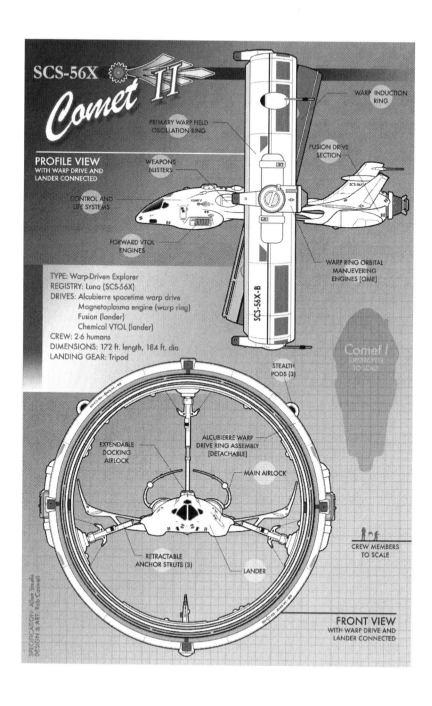

SCS-56X

Comet II

WARP INDUCTION RING

PRIMARY WARP FIELD OSCILLATION RING

PROFILE VIEW
WITH WARP DRIVE AND
LANDER CONNECTED

WEAPONS BLISTERS

FUSION DRIVE SECTION

CONTROL AND LIFE SYSTEMS

FORWARD VTOL ENGINES

WARP RING ORBITAL MANUEVERING ENGINES [OME]

SCS-56X-B

TYPE: Warp-Driven Explorer
REGISTRY: Luna (SCS-56X)
DRIVES: Alcubierre spacetime warp drive
Magnetoplasma engine (warp ring)
Fusion (lander)
Chemical VTOL (lander)
CREW: 2-6 humans
DIMENSIONS: 172 ft. length, 184 ft. dia
LANDING GEAR: Tripod

Comet I
DESTROYED
TO SCALE

STEALTH PODS (3)

EXTENDABLE DOCKING AIRLOCK

ALCUBIERRE WARP DRIVE RING ASSEMBLY [DETACHABLE]

MAIN AIRLOCK

CREW MEMBERS TO SCALE

RETRACTABLE ANCHOR STRUTS (3)

LANDER

FRONT VIEW
WITH WARP DRIVE AND
LANDER CONNECTED

SPECIFICATION: Allen Steele
DESIGN & ART: Rob Caswell

Interlude:
Marshall Gurney Reports

The airlock's sphincter door irised open, and Captain Future stepped through.

Pausing within the airlock's recessed alcove, he cautiously studied the catwalk outside the airlock, plasma-beam pistol raised and ready to fire at the first sign of trouble. The catwalk circled the interior wall of a large shaft, with a bridge-like walkway leading from it to the rotarvator, a rotating space tether that rose through the shaft core like an immense steel sequoia.

The scene was captured from above by a surveillance camera. No more than thirty feet from the airlock, three figures in vacuum suits – two men and a woman – crouched upon the walkway beside the rotarvator. Their attention was focused on the small package one of them was welding to the tether, so they didn't immediately spot Curt Newton as he cycled through the hatch behind them.

Curt's expression couldn't be discerned through the faceplate of his helmet, but Ezra Gurney had little doubt that it was tense with concentration. And although the image was in playback mode and not in real-time, Ezra couldn't help but feel apprehensive about the situation. This was a life or death scenario, and he knew that, in just a few moments, one of the people he was watching would die.

Ezra remembered the reason why he was reviewing the surveillance footage in the first place: to prepare a report for Halk Anders, the commandant of the Interplanetary Police Force and Ezra's superior. Anders was famously impatient with written reports, which he complained were long and over-detailed without really telling him much. And while Simon Wright, the Futureman sometimes known as the Brain, routinely wrote and submitted a mission report, Anders never read them, relying on Ezra to read them and send him a verbal summation instead.

Ezra often wondered if Anders was secretly semi-literate. Once, while reading a routine report Ezra had hand-delivered to his office, the head of Section 4 (Intelligence) had observed Anders moving his lips as he skimmed the printed pages. Ezra knew better than to tell anyone what he'd seen; instead, he resolved to make his verbal reports as dramatic and straight-forward as he could, the way Anders liked them.

Running a finger across his desk screen, Ezra froze the video playback. He'd forgotten where he'd last left off, so he skipped back about thirty seconds, then held a forefinger against the button in his left ear, touched the *Play* button, and listened again:

"*– rendezvoused with the Stratos Venera colony above Venus, where Simon Wright assisted Newton in covertly boarding the colony's mobile mining platform as its rotarvator was in descent mode through the planet's upper atmosphere. At the same time, the other two Futuremen, Otho and Grag, piloted the* Comet *toward the colony in low-orbit above the planet. The alleged Starry Messenger saboteurs were therefore unaware that Captain Future had tracked them to the open shaft at the center of Stratos, where he caught them affixing a low-yield dynatomite explosive device to the rotarvator ...*"

Ezra stopped the audio. Good, that sounded clear enough. "Hell," he muttered, "even Anders wouldn't have trouble understanding this."

Cut it out. He chided himself for showing disrespect for his superiors, even when no one else was around. Start doing this when you're alone, and before you know it, you're mouthing off to them in person. Not good. Ezra cleared his throat, checked his notes again, then touched the *Record* button and resumed his narrative.

"Once Curt –" pause; erase; start again "– once Special Agent Newton located the suspects, he made an effort to give them a chance to surrender, and didn't open fire until they first fired on him."

Ezra hit the *Stop* button, then resumed the video feed. On the screen, he watched as Curt took a few moments to observe the saboteurs. Ezra knew that, at this moment, Curt was having a brief consultation with the Brain, who was piloting the recon pod the two of them had used to travel down from the *Comet*. The ship was in low orbit near Venera, the colony's habitat; its mining platform, Stratos, was positioned at one end of a 1,630 kilometer space elevator that periodically rotated down into Venus's upper atmosphere. Their communications feed had been recorded as well, but Ezra didn't want to get his voice mixed up with Curt's and Simon's, so he left it out, and instead continued to watch as Curt emerged from the alcove, lowering his gun to aim straight at the suspected saboteurs.

The woman spotted Curt at once. Before he had a chance to demand their surrender, she pointed him out to her male companions. Before any of them had a chance to react, Curt opened fire.

An expanding wave of translucent plasma halos, resembling the smoke rings a tobacco addict might exhale, erupted from his gun, cascading across the distance to strike the explosive device the saboteurs had been attaching to the rotarvator. This needed to be explained, lest Anders come away with the impression that Curt had opened fire without first identifying himself or giving the perps a chance to drop their guns and give up.

Ezra paused the video again, then resumed his narration. "Please observe that, when Special Agent Newton fired on the suspects, he wasn't aiming at any one of them in particular, but at the explosive device they'd just finished rigging. His principal concern at that point was making sure that the bomb couldn't be detonated, either deliberately or by accident."

The firefight continued. The saboteurs had come armed and they had no qualms about exchanging fire with Captain Future. When Ezra reviewed the playback the first time, just a few minutes ago, he'd heard the comlink feed Curt's suit had picked up and recorded. So even as Curt took cover behind the catwalk railing, Ezra heard one of the men shout, "Goddammit, it's Captain Future! Shoot him!"

Ezra couldn't help but smile. He still thought "Captain Future" was one of the silliest names he'd ever heard, but there was no mistaking the fear in the suspect's voice. Over the past five years, Starry Messenger had learned to dread Captain Future and the Futuremen. If they'd ever laughed at Curt and his strange team, the laughter stopped after it came out that they'd been responsible for the annihilation of the Starry Messenger satrap on Mars, along with the extermination of the Sons of the Two Moons, the phony religious cult they'd created as a cover for their nefarious activities, and the death of their leader Ul Quorn, otherwise known as the Magician of Mars.

Even so, although the terrorist organization had been severely damaged by their showdown with Curt on Mars, Starry Messenger wasn't totally destroyed. Since then, they'd slowly picked up the pieces and rebuilt themselves, and now they were stronger than ever. Their objectives remained the same: the militant separation of Mars and the outer planet colonies from the Solar Coalition, along with the end of the generations-long effort to terraform Mars. Like outlaw separatist movements of the past – the Irish Republican Army, the Palestinian Liberation Organization, Free Luna – Starry Messenger would stop at nothing to achieve their goals. And although the liberation of Stratos Venera wasn't one of their objectives – aphrodites were one branch of *Homo cosmos* that remained content with belonging to SolCol – this unprecedented attempt to target the orbital tether that connected Stratos with Venera was a clear indication that Starry Messenger was no longer interested in respecting Venusian neutrality.

But this incident was something else entirely. And that was because of the identity of one of the terrorists involved.

As Ezra watched, Curt took down the saboteurs even though they outnumbered him three to one. The first guy took a direct hit from Curt's plasma-beam pistol, which had been set for stun: he collapsed on the walkway, where he lay until the IPF tactical squad Simon had summoned came down from Venera to take him into custody.

The second man wasn't so fortunate. He made it to the catwalk on the other side of the shaft, but then stopped to trade shots with Curt. When Curt clipped him, he didn't collapse unconscious on the catwalk, but instead toppled over the railing. There was nothing below to halt his plunge. Screaming, the terrorist plummeted down the open shaft and disappeared from sight. Below lay only the dense, acid-laden clouds of the Venusian atmosphere, an opaque and deadly veil that perpetually hid the planet's fiery surface from view. When the terrorist finally hit the ground, there would've been nothing left of him but a skeleton in a shredded skinsuit, and even that would probably have been incinerated.

Once more, Ezra paused the playback, then resumed his narration of what he'd just seen. He was careful to give Curt the benefit of the doubt and explain that the second terrorist's demise was entirely accidental; Curt had not intended to stun him in such a way that he'd fall over the railing to his death. As he spoke, Ezra reflected that it was remarkable that more outlaws, Starry Messenger terrorists or otherwise, hadn't died during their encounters with Captain Future and his crew. In his career as IPF's troubleshooter, Curt had always made an effort to take prisoners, not lives. Even when some of the people he'd pursued had done their best to kill him or the Futuremen, Curt seldom resorted to lethal measures. As a result, SolCol's maximum security prison on Pluto was full of people whom he'd brought to justice; they might resent Captain Future for putting them in a cell, but at least it wasn't a grave.

As Ezra continued to watch, Curt pursued the last of the three suspects. The woman had taken cover behind the rotarvator's massive cable; now she was running across the walkway on the other side of the tether, heading for the catwalk opposite where Curt stood. It was clear that she was heading for the elevator on the opposite side of the shaft; if she could reach it, she'd be able to ascend to Venera and lose herself within the colony's vast habitat.

Jumping over the unconscious saboteur he'd felled just moments earlier, Curt sprinted down the walkway after her. The woman saw him coming and stopped to take a pot-shot at him with the particle beam rifle she carried. But her aim was wild and, to Curt's credit, he didn't return her fire. As the Brain had stated in his written report, she was too close to the catwalk railing and he didn't want to repeat the same error he'd made with her second male companion.

The woman continued to run, and as soon as she reached the lift and hit the call button, he stopped, leveled his pistol, and drew a bead on her. Plasma rings rushed from the gun barrel; they hit the fleeing woman in the back just as the elevator doors opened. Stunned, she fell face-first to the catwalk's gridwork floor, her body half-in and half-out of the lift.

In no hurry, Curt strolled across the shaft, pausing long enough to briefly inspect the bomb and make sure that it no longer posed an imminent threat. The woman was still unconscious when Curt reached her. He punted the rifle out of her reach, then knelt beside her and gently pushed her over on her back so that he could see her face.

This was the part Ezra hadn't been looking forward to explaining. He touched the *Pause* button again, took a deep breath, then picked up where he'd left off.

"It was not until after Special Agent Newton apprehended the suspects that he discovered that he knew one of them...Ashi Lanyr, whom Newton had met about ten years ago when both of them were teenagers. Lanyr is an aphrodite and a lifelong Stratos Venera colonist, but has been living outside the law since adolescence, when she ran away from her parents just before they immigrated to Earth. Since then, she'd been subsisting as a professional thief until, just a short while ago, she joined the Starry Messenger cell on Stratos Venera and became involved in the plot to sabotage the rotarvator."

Ezra stopped for a moment to collect his thoughts, then went on. "Curt...Special Agent Newton, that is...was unaware of her identity until he made the arrest. Once he did, though, he insisted on bringing her in himself instead of turning her over to IPF officers on Stratos Venera. At the time of this report, Lanyr is in his custody aboard the *Comet*. Agent Newton and the Futuremen are transporting her to the Moon, where they intend to rendezvous with an IPF frigate and turn her over to them. Apparently, he wants to interrogate the suspect on his own, and given his earlier relationship with her, I'm allowing him to do so."

As he was speaking, Ezra heard his office door open behind him. He didn't look around, though, until he finished his last thought. When he finally turned his head, he saw who'd come in: Lt. Joan Randall, his senior officer and right-hand woman in Section 4.

"Oh…howdy, Joan!" Ezra turned away from her as quickly as he could. He knew that his face had just turned red, and he didn't want her wondering why.

"Hello, chief," Joan said. Although he couldn't see her either, Ezra knew that she must be looking over his shoulder at his desk screen. "Making your report to Anders?"

"Yup. Part of the job I hate the most…giving Halk his damn report." Without being aware of it, Ezra had slipped into a subconscious mannerism of his: reverting to the looney accent and diction that he normally used when speaking to friends and colleagues, but didn't use on formal occasions. Native-born selenites like himself – a.k.a. looneys – were proud of their Texas heritage, but often it made them self-conscious about the hayseed impression it tended to project.

"I see…I see." Joan slowly nodded; when Ezra glanced at her again, she was still gazing at the image frozen on his screen. "And have you told Ezra who that woman is? Ashi Lanyr, I mean."

Damn it. She'd read Simon's report, too. Ezra looked away again. "What makes you think he'd be interested in –?"

"I've known Curt for a long time now," Joan said quietly, "and so have you. If this woman is someone he once cared about, that's going to have an impact on the charges IPF is going to bring against her, don't you think?"

"Now looky here, gal –"

Ezra was saved by a sharp beep from his desk. A glance at the screen confirmed what it was: a priority message from IPF Central Command. And speak of the devil, who would it happen to be but Anders himself; the Commandant's ID and confirmation numbers were on the screen below a thumbnail of his face.

"Anders," Ezra said, looking at Joan again. "Can you excuse me? Looks like it's for my eyes only."

"Sure, of course." Joan took a couple of steps back, but as the door opened for her, she paused for a moment. "But we still need to talk about this, chief."

"I won't forget." Ezra forced a smile. "Now shoo... I gotta see what the ol' man wants." Which was ironic, because Ezra was a few years older than Anders, who'd been a rookie when Ezra was already a senior officer. But Halk Anders knew how to play the game while Ezra Gurney, preferring active duty over a desk job, had steadfastly refused promotion to administrative jobs. So, Ezra had a boss who was younger and a little less experienced, but outranked him nonetheless. It didn't always make for a comfortable working relationship.

As soon as the door closed behind Joan, Ezra took the call. "Hello, sir," he said as Anders appeared on-screen. "I was just about to wrap up the report on the Stratos Venera case, if that's what you're wondering."

"It's not." Anders' bulldog face had the perpetually displeased expression of a humorless man who seldom smiled and therefore went through life glowering at the world and everyone who lived in it. "But I hope you're going to tell me that Newton and his crew are on their way back home. Something's come up, and we need them at once."

"The *Comet* left Venus just a little while ago," Ezra said. "They should be landing at Tycho in just an hour or so. I can contact them...what should I tell 'em?"

"Remember the *Titan King*?" Anders asked. "The space liner that was hijacked near Saturn a few months ago?" Ezra nodded and Anders went on. "It's turned up again ... and you'll won't believe where."

THE GUNS OF PLUTO

The Return of Ul Quorn, Book II

by Allen Steele

I

If there is a Hell in the solar system, it's Venus. And if there's a Purgatory, it's Pluto.

The largest minor planet in the Kuiper Belt is so distant from the planets of the inner system – an average distance of nearly six billion miles from the Sun, about forty times farther than Earth – it takes over nine hours for a radio or laser communications transmission to be received there. Its highly eccentric orbit at a 17.4-degree angle above and below the solar plane of the ecliptic makes Pluto a difficult world to reach; since Hohmann transfer maneuvers or similar gravity-assist trajectories are useless, deep-space vessels have to expend more energy to get there.

And it's **cold**. Pluto's distance from the Sun, along with its sparse atmosphere, gives it a maximum surface temperature of -369^{0}F. Atmospheric nitrogen, methane and carbon dioxide freeze solid on the ground; the terrain is largely comprised of volatile ices the color of pink and brown-tinted snow. The Sun is little more than a luminous spot in the sky that Pluto takes 248 years to orbit; any warmth it casts, even in what amounts to summertime during perihelion, is negligible.

While Pluto is frigid beyond belief, though, it isn't dead.

The most prominent geographic feature of its southern hemisphere is a vast, heart-shaped region known as the Tombaugh Regio. Named after the twentieth century astronomer who discovered Pluto – and famously made the mistake of believing that it was an actual planet, an error that wasn't corrected for another seventy years – it stands out not only for its peculiar shape, but also its flatness. From orbit, the Tombaugh Regio resembles an icy desert surrounded by mountains, hills and craters, unscarred by the meteor strikes and subsurface geological activity that have molded most of this little world.

The northwest side of the region is an enormous lowland area known as the Sputnik Planitia. Like the rest of the Tombaugh Regio, it was formed by an ancient collision with some large space object, probably another Kuiper Belt asteroid. Although most of Pluto's surface is comprised of ice-covered rock, the Sputnik Planitia is a sea of frozen nitrogen with island-size icebergs floating near the shore. Deep beneath hundreds of feet of volatile ice lies a subsurface ocean of liquid water polluted by ammonia, heated by geological activity at the planetary core.

This ocean makes Pluto desirable for practical reasons. H_2O in liquid form is one of the most valuable resources of the solar system's outer worlds. The vast natural reservoir beneath the Tombaugh Regio is estimated to be more than 100 kilometers in diameter and up to 150 kilometers thick. Neptune's watery mantle is larger and deeper, of course, but not nearly as accessible; it would take enormous kinetic energy to achieve escape velocity from that gas giant, while Pluto's low mass and slow rotation give it a surface gravity of only .08g.

Pluto's reservoirs may be distant, but at least they're accessible. When humankind began to colonize the solar system, the Kuiper Belt became an invaluable resource, with Pluto the most desirable of the minor planets. But who would live in such a harsh and distant place?

Adventurers, outcasts, madmen…and prisoners.

The Sputnik Planitia Penal Colony is situated within an immense iceberg that ascended to the top of the Tombaugh Regio's frozen ocean many thousands of years ago. Since it is comprised of water ice with traces of ammonia and pieces of rock brought up from the bottom of the hidden sea, the iceberg is lighter than the "dry ice" surrounding it and therefore floats on the surface. It moves, but very, very slowly. Permanently locked within the frozen expanse, the berg has remained in place for countless millennia, its lateral movement measurable only in inches over the course of centuries.

When the Solar Coalition decided to build a maximum security prison on Pluto sixty-seven years ago, the government reduced construction costs by using native materials as much as possible. Once terran and arisian surveyors located a suitable iceberg, SolCol dispatched a crew of jovian civil engineers and Grag construction 'bots to the site of the new prison: below the equator within sight of the Zheng He mountains, just off the coast of Viking Terra, the nearest continent.

Men from Jupiter and robots from Ohio labored for many months; when they were done, the iceberg no longer resembled its natural form. It now looks like an irregular stack of white tesseracts carved from native ice, with solarium domes, solar farms and dish antennae scattered here and there across the flat rooftops. From the center of the tesseracts rise the silver cylinders of the prison's freshwater distillery; along the northern outer wall are a row of spherical water tanks, all heated to keep their contents from freezing solid.

Sprawling across the iceberg, the prison resembles a jumble of toys left behind by a giant child. Its benign surface appearance masks the fact that most of the prison is located within labyrinthine warrens carved inside the iceberg below the surface of the surrounding frozen sea. Within its glacial outer walls is a maze of cell blocks, enclosed courtyards, dining rooms, and crafts shops reinforced by slabs of native granite six inches thick, which in turn are insulated by hardened graphene foam impregnated with heating elements and electrical systems. With power supplied by fusion reactors, the result is an immense, habitable iceberg, impregnable from the outside and virtually impossible to break through from the inside.

The prison's landing field is located a short distance away, its small fleet of spacecraft resting within hangars resembling enormous igloos. The fleet includes freighters that periodically make sorties to low orbit, where they rendezvous with the giant tanker-ships arriving to transport distilled Plutonian water to the inner system. Pluto is helping a dead planet come back to life, for as Mars is gradually terraformed, its dry oceans and underground aquifers are being replenished by Pluto's water. The resources of the entire solar system are being tapped to transform Mars into an Earth-like planet; like Luna, Venus, and the moons of Jupiter and Saturn, Pluto has a role to fill in this epic undertaking.

Light gleams through barred windows scattered across the prison's cube-like sections, with tubular enclosed walkways leading from one tesseract to another. A few large, fortified entrances are located at ground level, including a main entrance that resembles the drawbridge of a medieval castle. As a matter of procedure, these doors are kept locked. Likewise, robot sentries ceaselessly patrol the prison's interior. However, these precautions are almost unnecessary, for another sort of sentinel stands watch outside the prison walls.

Arranged in a broad circle surrounding the iceberg on all four sides are a collection of X-shaped cruciforms, each seven feet tall, crudely fashioned from pieces of scrap metal.

Lashed to each one is a human skeleton.

There's little difference whether they're *Homo sapiens* or *Homo cosmos*, terran, aphrodite, aresian, or jovian. Each has been stripped of flesh, and if one were to examine them closely, you might see that their cold, bleached bones have tiny nicks and abrasions, the sort that can only be left behind by razor-sharp knives.

None of the skeletons have a name by which they can be identified, but that's not necessary. Every living person here knows who they are: convicts, the remains of individuals who'd once been fellow inmates, friends, or lovers in this loveless place. The black holes of eye sockets stare back at those who meet their sightless gaze, and if anyone inside the prison walls happens to forget why the skeletons are there, a signboard at the feet of the corpse nearest the main entrance is a subtle reminder:

> *If You're Thinking of Leaving,*
> *Please Come Over For Dinner...*
> *We Would Love To Have You!*

Dry witticism, courtesy of one of the kuiperians who live in the nearby mountains and work at the prison. It's often difficult to know which the inmates dread more: being caught out in the open, where the blood would literally freeze in your veins within seconds, or falling into the hands of a kuiperian who hasn't eaten well lately.

The Sputnik Planitia Penal Colony has another name: Cold Hell. And like the mythical Hell, once a man or woman is banished to this place, there is no returning home.

Or so it is believed.

II

A t approximately the same time that Captain Future's ship, the *Comet II,* was going into orbit around Venus and Curt Newton was preparing for his mission to Stratos Venera, two men on the other side of the solar system were enjoying a quiet game of chess in the penal colony's monitor room.

Located in a wheel-shaped turret atop the prison, the monitor room was the nerve center of Cold Hell, the place from which prison staff could monitor every corner of the penitentiary. The monitor room was staffed round the clock of the prison's Earth-standard 24-hour sol (as opposed to Pluto's own day, which was six times longer) with at least one person present at all times.

This morning, two men were on duty: Edward Jeerdin, the prison's chief warden, and Omar bin-Nerrivik, the hulking jovian who happened to be on watch that particular shift. Seated on a stool at a round table, hands clasped together beneath his chin as he studied the chessboard, Jeerdin wasn't the sort of person one might imagine as being in charge of the solar system's toughest pen. Earth-born and slight of build, he had the soft-spoken demeanor of the professional bureaucrat.

On the other hand, it was hard to imagine that the brooding, red-bearded giant seated across the table from him was a chess master, let alone one who'd won several system-wide competitions and for whom a complex stratagem, "Omar's Gambit," was christened. Omar bin-Nerrivik was a hard man and formidable chess player. Being a prison guard was just a job; the game was his life.

Which was why Ed Jeerdin's favorite part of the day was the hour or two he spent each morning with Omar. Jeerdin became the prison's warden only reluctantly – a long story in itself, involving bureaucratic politics and his failure to understand how they worked – and might have died of boredom a long time ago had he not discovered Omar's hidden talents. Jeerdin was no mean chess player himself, but next to the big jovian he was little more than a novice who'd just learned how to castle...and he loved it. Never once had he ever defeated Omar, but having such an unbeatable opponent was a challenge.

As for Omar, there were times when he imagined curling up a fist, reaching across the table, and with one mighty blow pile-driving the warden's head and neck down between his shoulders. He didn't know if he could really do that, but it would be fun to try. Jeerdin played the sloppiest, most disorganized game Omar had ever seen. Were it not for the fact that the warden was his boss, the hulking guard would have stopped playing with him a long time ago. But he seemed to be stuck with this artless dilettante as a regular opponent, so Omar let Jeerdin pretend that he was actually making a three-time winner of the Ganymede Prize sweat a bit, and refrained from trouncing him in five or six moves.

The warden had just done something truly stupid, moving his queen's knight to take out one of Omar's pawns while unwittingly leaving the queen herself wide open for counter-attack, when there was a sharp treble from the master console behind him. A moment later, the pleasant female voice of Sharon, Cold Hell's AI, came through their headsets: "Pardon the interruption, gentlemen, but the orbital sentinel has detected a spacecraft entering Pluto's gravitational sphere of influence."

Sharon could only speak to them verbally. Cold Hell's com system broadcast a dampening field that disabled Anni implants, thus preventing the inmates from using their neural nets to secretly plot escapes or uprisings. Jeerdin had become so accustomed to hearing Sharon's voice, though, that he didn't look up from the board.

"Freighter?" he asked, speaking aloud. "We've got one coming soon, don't we?" He grimaced as he spoke; five seconds after removing his hand from his knight, it occurred to him that he'd made a strategic error.

Omar glanced at the whiteboard on the wall above them. The schedule for incoming and outgoing spacecraft had been drawn there. "Not for three more weeks," he murmured, his hairy eyebrows knitting together.

"That is correct, Omar," Sharon said. "The next spacecraft scheduled for arrival is the SCS tanker *Larry Niven*, and it won't get here for three weeks, two days, and twenty-one hours."

Neither Jeerdin or Omar said anything for a couple of moments. Their minds were still hovering between the game they were playing and the unexpected arrival of an unknown spacecraft. Still staring at the board, Jeerdin asked, "What's the transponder ID?"

"There is no transponder signal, Warden," Sharon said. "I'm receiving no telemetry from the vessel, only a lidar return"

Jeerdin finally raised his eyes. "No transponder? Have you attempted to contact the ship?"

"Not yet. Would you like for me to attempt to open a comlink channel?"

"Yes, please."

Sitting up straight, Jeerdin adjusted his headset's mike wand, crossed his arms, and waited. From the corridor outside, there came the steady mechanical stomp of oversized metal feet. A sentry 'bot walked past the door, particle beam rifle cradled in its arms. It paused for a moment, its skull-like head turning to let its narrow eyes swept the room. Finding nothing unusual, it continued on its way. Neither man so much as glanced in its direction. A couple of seconds later, there was a soft chime, announcing that the Ku-band transceiver was active.

"Unidentified spacecraft," Jeerdin said aloud, "this is Sputnik Planitia Penal Colony, Chief Warden Edward Jeerdin speaking. Our satellites have monitored you entering Pluto's sphere of influence. Be advised that this is a secure zone and that unauthorized orbital insertions or surface landings are strictly forbidden. Please respond at once, do you copy?"

As he spoke, Omar pushed his swivel chair away from the board and into the center of the horseshoe-shaped master control station. A glance at the holo display above the center console confirmed what Sharon had just told them: a blinking red spot had appeared at the outer edge of the spherical wire-frame plotting board surrounding Pluto. The red spot was coming within range of the nearest of a ring of orange spots signifying the sentinel satellites in equatorial orbit around the planetoid.

Omar flipped a series of toggle switches; with a double-beep, the spots changed from orange to green, and dotted lines ran to the red spot from the three sats closest to it. "Defense system armed and locked on. Now on manual control, awaiting your orders." He rested his massive right hand beside the fire-control button.

Jeerdin nodded. For the moment, the chess game had been forgotten. "I repeat, incoming spacecraft, this is —"

"We copy, Sputnik Planitia PC." The voice that came over the comlink was male and aresian-accented. "This is the liner *Titan King*, chief communications officer Kars Kaastro speaking."

Jeerdin's mouth fell open, and there was astonishment on Omar's normally taciturn face. Everyone in the system had heard about the hijacking and subsequent disappearance of the *Titan King*. That happened just over three months ago; the spaceliner's fate had been an unsolved mystery since then.

"What in Io's flaming —?" Omar began.

"*Titan King*, we read you." At once, Jeerdin was on his feet. In two quick steps, he was standing beside Omar, both men staring up at the holo. "Can you confirm your identity, please? We're not receiving transponder telemetry from you."

Another moment passed. "We copy, Warden. Our transponder was destroyed when the *King* was taken over by pirates. It wasn't until just a few days ago that the remaining members of the crew retook control of the ship. We're declaring an emergency and requesting permission to enter low orbit. Please respond at once."

"Who's in command, Mr. Kaastro?"

"Harl al-Sarakka is the senior bridge officer. He has assumed command. Captain Lamont is dead, killed by the hijackers."

Jeerdin glanced at Omar. The helmsman's surname indicated that he was another jovian; sure enough, Omar nodded. "I know him," he said quietly. "His clan and mine are joined, and we walked like men together."

The warden understood. Jovian clans joined through the marriage of individual members, matrimonial oaths assuring that their members would treat one another as cousins thereafter. Furthermore, when young men in this aggressively male-dominated society reached the age of maturity, they entered an intensive period of survival training in which they learned how to cope with the merciless cold of Callisto, culminating in wilderness treks where the only two possible outcomes were life or death. Thus the bands of jovian boys who "walked like men together" across the plains of Valhalla shared a bond making them as close as blood-brothers.

So Omar bin-Nerrivik knew that he could trust Harl al-Sarakka. Which meant that Jeerdin better do so, too, for telling a jovian that you didn't trust a clan mate was…well, the warden didn't think he'd like having a chess piece shoved down his throat.

"Proceed," he said softly.

Omar nodded again, then tapped his headset's mic wand. "Harl of Sarakka, this is Omar of Nerrivik. Greetings, cousin. You've been gone for too long."

"Greetings, brother and cousin," came the reply. "I have been missing for quite a while, yes, but now I've returned. It has been a long journey. Will you not welcome me and my shipmates?"

Omar looked at Jeerdin. "This is indeed Harl al-Sarakka," he murmured. "Only another of my kind would speak this way." Jeerdin nodded and Omar resumed the conversation with the *Titan King*'s helmsman. "Of course," he went on, a little more warmth in his voice. "Nonetheless, I'd still like to know where you've been and what has happened."

A pause. "All your questions will be answered, fellow of the walk," Harl al-Sarakka said, "but it is a long story and our immediate needs are great. Will you allow the *Titan King* to make an emergency landing on your field? It was severely damaged during our efforts to retake control from the pirates, and the life support system is presently in critical condition."

"Just one moment, cousin, and I will ask if this is possible."

Omar turned to Jeerdin; no reason to repeat what he'd just heard. The warden absently gazed at the nearby chess board, studying the pieces without really seeing them. He had little doubt that Cold Hell would be able to accommodate an emergency landing by the *Titan King*. The liner was one of the largest vessels in space, but the Plutonian icepack was miles thick near the prison, the landing field itself was concrete-reinforced with ice freighters in mind, and Pluto's nitrogen-carbon dioxide atmosphere was thin enough and its surface gravity sufficiently low to allow for atmospheric entry and landing by a spacecraft the size of the *King*.

So the spaceliner **could** land there; the real question was whether it **should**. There were very strict regulations for which vessels could make planetfall at Cold Hell, and although emergency landings were permitted, the people who'd written those rules believed that freighters, prison barges, or shuttles would be the kind of vessels most likely to do so. No one had ever dreamed that a passenger liner last seen in orbit above Saturn would find its way to the remote and untouristed Kuiper Belt.

By the book, Jeerdin knew that he should first contact the IPF, the Interplanetary Police Force under whose authority Cold Hell operated, and ask for their advice and permission. But that was impractical. Not only would it take about nine hours for a radio signal to reach Earth, but then his message would have to work its way up the chain of command to Halk Anders, the IPF commandant who'd have the final word. And then it would take another nine hours for his response to reach Pluto. This meant that almost an entire sol would go by before the stricken liner would know whether it could touch down. If the situation aboard the *Titan King* was as dire as Harl al-Sarakka made it sound, lives could be lost in the meantime.

Fortunately, the warden had been granted a lot of autonomy in how he ran the Sputnik Planitia Penal Colony. So long as the inmates were kept in line, he could do pretty much what he wanted.

And having a role in the recovery of the *Titan King* couldn't hurt his record. It might even help get him out of the freezing ass-end of the solar system and back to the warm and civilized worlds closer to the Sun.

He leaned back against the console and, confidently folding his arms across his chest, spoke aloud. "*Titan King*, this is Warden Edward Jeerdin. You have permission for an emergency landing on our field."

Another moment passed, then the voice of communications officer Kars Kaastro returned. "We copy, Warden Jeerdin. Thank you. Please open your traffic control system to allow for our nav comp to link with it."

"Wilco, *Titan King*. Stand by for downlink."

Jeerdin bent over a keypad on the console. He quickly entered the necessary password that would allow him access to the penal colony's communications network, then entered the codes that would let the *Titan King*'s flight control system link with the prison network. This would help Harl al-Sarakka plot the liner's atmospheric entry and touchdown, tasks difficult to achieve without computer assistance at both ends.

Several seconds passed. Then, without warning, all the lights in the prison went dark.

III

The cyberattack began with a Trojan-horse program that piggybacked its way into Cold Hell's comp net via the communications uplink with the *Titan King*. When Jeerdin entered the passwords that gave the liner direct interface with the penitentiary, he unwittingly opened the pen to an assault via its cybernetic infrastructure.

The blackout was just the first act. Although the prison's most vital life-support systems, its atmosphere and heat generators, were left untouched, lights throughout both the aboveground structures and the subsurface warrens were extinguished. So was power to all terminals and interfaces, including Sharon.

Cold Hell was just beginning its day. Throughout its cell blocks and dining halls and shower rooms, the enclosed exercise yard and the freshwater distillery, the library and the infirmary and the hydroponics greenhouse, voices were raised in surprised outrage as the lights went out. The men and women from a half-dozen worlds who comprised the prison population – 1,859 inmates, 156 staff members – had learned to get through the tedium of their lives by adopting predictable daily patterns and schedules where anything out of the ordinary was unwanted. So the blackout, an unprecedented incident that even the lifers couldn't recall ever happening before, upset the prison's inhabitants more than it would have on the outside. The sharper inmates immediately realized that something very unusual was about to happen.

Five seconds later, it did.

Most of Cold Hell's guards were neither *Homo sapiens* nor *Homo cosmos,* but robots: Grag S-250p and S-290p sentry 'bots, second-cousins to Curt Newton's lifelong companion, the Futureman simply known as Grag. Although designed to be autonomous, the prison's sixty-five guard 'bots were linked to one another via their own comp net, which in turn was controlled by Sharon. So while the 'bots were capable of acting independently, they could also perform as a single unit if and when new primary instructions came down the line.

Which is what happened.

Inside the monitor room, barely ten seconds had passed when, from a short distance down the corridor, Edward Jeerdin and Omar bin-Nerrivik heard the steady, mechanical stamp of feet. The 'bot who'd walked by a few minutes ago was returning. Neither of them paid attention; smothered and confused by the sudden darkness, the terran warden and the jovian guard fumbled blindly at lifeless consoles in a bewildered effort to restore power. Power was control in Cold Hell; without power, there was no control over the inmates. And if they got loose…

Omar's eyes were better suited for seeing in the dark. He'd just located the master control panel when he heard the approaching robot. Two glowing red eyes appeared in the doorway, the only source of illumination they'd seen in the last dozen or so seconds.

"Oh, thank God," Jeerdin said. "Come over here and –"

A scarlet particle beam from the rifle in the robot's hands silently ripped through the room, a murderous scythe that sliced through both men. Jeerdin crumpled to the floor; Omar fell across the chess board, scattering the pieces. They were dead before they knew what happened.

So were dozens of other staffers – guards, supervisors, clerical and maintenance workers, cooks, the prison doctor and his nursing assistants – scattered throughout Cold Hell. The prison's comp net was designed to track everyone by the subcutaneous transponders with which they were injected upon arrival and provide a constantly updated map of their current whereabouts. This included the staff members as well as the inmates. So the 'bots knew at once where all the screws were; they located the closest ones and immediately turned their guns on them.

The prisoners took cover as best they could, throwing themselves behind furniture if there was any nearby or flat against the floor if there wasn't. They needn't have bothered. The annihilation was as precise as it was complete; anyone whose transponders identified them as an inmate was ignored or avoided.

Within three minutes, everyone in Cold Hell who wasn't wearing an orange jumpsuit lay dead, tracked down and wiped out by the sentry 'bots.

For several long seconds, the prison was utterly silent. Then the inmates slowly rose to their feet. They were confused, terrified, and incredulous, and not one of them knew what had just happened or why.

But someone did.

IV

"Orbital insertion burn, sixty secs and counting." Harl al-Sarakka's hands roamed the helm console, making fine adjustments. "All stations, rig for turnaround. 179 degrees to port, on my mark." Without looking away from his console, he spoke to the man sitting behind him in the captain's chair. "Main engine on standby, sir. Firing on your mark."

"Fire when ready, Mr. al-Sarakka. I'll trust your judgment." The Black Pirate had once again donned the dark apparel from which he derived his name, including the mask that hid his features. Everyone aboard the liner had seen his face by now, of course, but it wasn't for them that he disguised himself. He was about to make the next move in a complex game, and he wasn't ready to reveal his identity just yet.

Through the red lenses of his mask, he watched the forward bridge screen. It displayed a rear-angle view of the ship's stern. Pluto loomed behind the engine cluster, the heart-shaped Tombaugh Regio coming into view over the eastern horizon. Even in the wan light of the distant sun, the surrounding hills and mountains were visible, casting shadows across an ocean of pale pink ice. But he didn't get a chance to admire the view before Harl al-Sarakka reached zero in his silent countdown and pushed six buttons on his board.

The six fusion main engines silently flared, and a shudder passed through the command center as the vessel formerly christened the *Titan King* began its deceleration burn. In the three months that had passed since the events of New Year's Eve, the immense liner had undergone a transformation. Just as the pirates of old Earth had taken the sailing vessels they'd seized and stripped them down to the bare boards to increase their speed under sail, the Black Pirate's crew – which now included the twelve *Titan King* crew members who'd accepted his invitation to join – had dismantled and jettisoned nearly every unessential item aboard the ship. If the IPF had known what the pirates were doing, they would've been able to locate the hijacked liner by simply following the trail of cabin furniture, recreational equipment, dinner dishes, silverware, lounge chairs, and holo projectors that had gone out the airlock (food and the contents of the ship's liquor cabinets were kept, though).

The most obvious change was that the forward observation dome was missing. The transparent hemisphere in which weightless dancers had performed surreal pirouettes no longer existed. Its glass panes were in the debris trail; workmen in spacesuits had spent most of the last twelve weeks cutting apart the metal frame and refashioning its pieces into something completely different, a large cradle-like structure whose purpose was not obvious.

With its many alterations, the ship could no longer be called a passenger liner. Which was just as well, because with its new purpose, it now had a new name. The *Titan King* was no more; in its place was the *Liberator*. Appropriately, the embossed metal flags of the Solar Coalition had been removed from the bow and midship fuselage; in their place was a circle with a pair of small horns protruding from its upper hemisphere – the ancient astrological sign for the planet Mercury, adopted in recent times as the symbol for Starry Messenger. The same symbol was now painted across bulkheads throughout the ship, along with the command center's walls.

Harl al-Sarakka let the engines continue their burn for the next ninety seconds as he intently watched his instruments. Around the wedge-shaped command center, other members of the bridge crew did the same. Some were hijackers who'd come aboard the *Liberator* on New Year's Eve and taken control of the space liner while it was in orbit above Saturn's rings, while others were like al-Sarakka, members of the *Titan King* crew who'd accepted the Black Pirate's invitation to join their cause.

The big jovian had been the first member of the *Titan King's* bridge crew to change colors. Like most of the others, his reasons were political, the long-standing grudge the inhabitants of the outer system harbored for the Solar Coalition. The Black Pirate was pleased when al-Sarakka was the first bridge officer to join; the giant helmsman had the respect of other senior crew members that the pirate needed, so when al-Sarakka came over to his side, most of those others promptly followed his example.

It was because of their cooperation that the Black Pirate had made good on his promise. Harl al-Sarakka and the others didn't know it, but if they hadn't joined the pirates, their leader would have killed Captain Lamont, then First Officer Watts, and then begun working his way down the list of non-essential personnel until he got what he wanted. The Black Pirate kept his word, though. Henri Lamont was retained because the buccaneer needed him, but Eliza Watts, ship's doctor Sean Dacus, and other crew members were allowed to join the passengers in the lifeboats.

The lifeboats were jettisoned shortly before the liner's trajectory took it around the far side of Saturn. Once the big ship was far enough away, the Black Pirate instructed al-Sarakka to plot a new course for the Kuiper Belt and fire the main engines. And so began the long journey to Pluto.

"Orbital insertion maneuver complete," al-Sarakka said. "Shutting down engines now." Without waiting for his new captain to give his assent, the helmsman rested his big hands on the main engine throttle-bars. Slowly, he pulled them back to the neutral position. With a low groan, another shudder passed through the ship. Then, silence. Al-Sarakka checked their position on the plotting board above his station. "Equatorial orbit achieved, 650 kilometers."

"Thank you, Mr. al-Sarakka. Well done." The Black Pirate leaned toward the helm station as far as his seat's belt-strap would let him. "And Harl?" he added, speaking quietly so that only the jovian could hear him. "Thank you for your assistance with…that other matter. I know that wasn't easy for you, but I hope you know just how necessary it was."

Harl al-Sarakka gave a silent nod of acknowledgment. It had taken a lot of talk over the past three months for the Black Pirate to persuade al-Sarakka that betraying another jovian – in particular Omar bin-Nerrivik, whom the pirate knew from Starry Messenger intelligence reports to have a tribal-bond relationship with the helmsman – was both unavoidable and necessary. It was only because Harl had convinced Omar that the *Titan King's* emergency was legitimate that the Black Pirate was able to eliminate Cold Hell's warden, staff, and guards, including Omar bin-Nerrivik himself.

The hulking jovian turned back to his station without another word, and the Black Pirate eyed him pensively. Harl al-Sarakka would have to be watched carefully; at the first sign of showing that his conscience was bothering him, he'd have to be liquidated as well.

The pirate chief then turned to Kars Kaastro, the aresian communications officer. "How goes the situation on the ground? What are the 'bots doing?"

"The sentry 'bots?" Kaastro shrugged. One of the screens at his station displayed a status grid for the AI system controlling the prison's robot sentries. The program N'Rala had given him just a little while ago enabled him to access this as well. "A few are taking out what's left of the prison staff. All the others are standing down."

"And the inmates?"

Another shrug. "Hard to tell. All I know is what I'm getting from the 'bots' vid feed. Look –"

The com officer ran a couple of fingers across his console touchpad and the video bank above the captain's chair displayed 'bot's-eye views of Cold Hell's subsurface warrens. Bodies lay were they'd fallen: plenty of blue uniforms, but no orange jumpsuits.

"I don't see any inmates," Kaastro said. "Nobody must have gotten in the way of the 'bots, so they must have gone into hiding."

"I'm sure we'll find them once we go down there." The Black Pirate sat up a little in the chair. "All right, let's roll with the next phase. Align the com laser for live transmission back to Luna. Time to shake somebody's tree."

Kaastro nodded and turned to his console again, and the Black Pirate reached up to his right ear and touched the prong he wore beneath his mask. "Oliver?" he asked, speaking to another member of his crew elsewhere aboard the *Liberator*. "Please find Captain Lamont in his cabin and bring him up to the command center."

"Yes, sir. What should I tell him?

"If he asks, tell him that the time has come for him to perform his role in all this...and he damned well better be persuasive."

V

Twelve hours and thirty-six minutes later, on the other side of the solar system, Curt Newton climbed up the ladder to the *Comet's* flight deck to have Otho turn to him from the co-pilot's seat and say, "Chief? Priority signal from Tycho…just came in."

"Joan?" Curt glanced past the android to the oval panes of the cockpit's wraparound windows. The Moon was already visible, a mottled gray orb three-quarters full, the slightly smaller Earth half-hiding behind it. The *Comet* was almost home; in just a few minutes, the ship would drop out of warp and begin deceleration maneuvers. "What's so important that it can't wait till we're on the ground?"

"I dunno. Ask her yourself, why don't you?" Otho smiled, a sardonic curling of bloodless lips on a pale white face. "While you're at it, you can tell her about your old girlfriend. I'm sure she's going to want to meet her."

"Not funny." Curt shot him a dark look as he unclipped his headset from his belt and fastened it over his uncombed red hair. "Are we on an open channel?" he asked, and Otho nodded. "Captain Future here, Tycho Base. What's going on?"

A brief, three-second pause, then: "Captain Future, this is an IPF Priority-A communique." Joan Randall's tone was clipped, all-business and no-nonsense. "Please switch to scrambler channel B-for-bravo, over."

"Wilco." Curt gave Otho another look. No longer smirking, Otho nodded and reached up to the com panel. A double-beep in Curt's ears told him that the *Comet's* radio comlink with Tycho Base was now being scrambled at both ends; no one else in cislunar space should be able to eavesdrop on them now. "Go ahead, Joan. I'm listening."

Another pause. "Curt, we've got a problem on Pluto. IPF Deep Space Com has received a message from Cold Hell. It would appear that a prison break is in progress."

"Uh-oh…sounds serious." In three quick steps, Curt was across the flight deck and sliding into the left-side pilot's chair. "Who sent the message, Ed Jeerdin?" He'd met Cold Hell's warden a couple of years ago when Jeerdin, who'd just been tapped to be the prison's new warden, had come to IPF's Luna headquarters on official business and Captain Future happened to be there at the same time. Not a close friend, but someone Curt knew and respected all the same.

"No," Joan replied. "Jeerdin's dead, or at least that's what the person who sent the message is claiming. Too much to explain, but –" another pause, this time not caused by transmission distance "– well, remember the *Titan King*, the liner that was hijacked earlier this year?"

"Think I've forgotten?" Curt and Otho traded a look. The hijacking and subsequent disappearance of the *King* was one of those rare mysteries they'd been unable to solve. It annoyed them that Captain Future and the Futuremen hadn't closed that particular case. "What's that got to do with it?"

"The *King* is back," Joan said. "And it appears that whoever was behind the hijacking is also responsible for the prison uprising."

"The Black Pirate?" Otho leaned forward in his seat, emerald-green eyes alert. "That son of a bitch is –?"

"We'll come straight in, Joan." Curt cut Otho off before he got wound up. The android was incensed that someone could elude identification by the simple trick of wearing a mask. Yet even though over a dozen crewmen from the *Titan King* had seen the Black Pirate before he and the hijackers let all but a few crewmen board the lifeboats, not one had been able to identify either the pirate leader or anyone else involved in the hijacking.

No one, that is, except the *Titan King's* executive officer, Eliza Watts. She alone had been able to supply IPF investigators with a good description of the tall young aresian woman who'd been the first person to disembark from the kronite shuttle that sent a phony distress call to the *King* and subsequently caused the liner to bring the smaller craft aboard. A woman who, if the description accurately matched someone Curt, Joan, and the Futuremen had met years ago, was supposed to be dead...

Curt shook off the thought. Now was not the time to speculate. "Joan, contact the IPF ship that's supposed to rendezvous with us. Tell them we're proceeding to Tycho instead and that we'll hand over our prisoner there. Is Ezra with you?"

"He's on his way from Descartes and says he'll take charge of the suspect once you arrive."

"Good. See you in a few. *Comet* over and out." Curt switched off the com, then let out his breath as he settled back in his seat. "Man...never get a break, do we?"

"You want a vacation?" Otho asked.

Curt rubbed his eyes. "I wouldn't mind one, no."

"Okay...hey, let's go to Venus!" Otho snapped his fingers. "I hear it's a lovely place."

Curt gave him a long, penetrating stare. "Get us out of warp, you jerk," he growled, "and don't say another word."

VI

A few minutes later, Otho collapsed the *Comet's* warp bubble. As soon as the sleek little ship came out of warp, Curt took manual control and performed the 180-degree long-axis rotation that turned the *Comet* about so that it was traveling stern-first toward the Moon, which by then was only 20,000 miles away. He then fired the fusion engines at full thrust, further decelerating the ship.

The *Comet's* artificial gravity faded along with the warp bubble; everyone aboard was strapped in, including the young woman being held in the locked cabin on the lower deck, so they were prepared for the prolonged surge that pushed them back in their couches and the zero-g that followed. The only persons aboard physically unaffected were Grag and the Brain, but even then, the robot and the cyborg made sure that they were secure before the maneuvers began.

By the time Curt throttled down the engines, the *Comet* was in orbit above the Moon. He and Otho decided to leave the warp torus in equatorial orbit. The *Comet* wouldn't be at Tycho Base for long, so there was no need to bring the entire ship down, as they occasionally did for dry-dock maintenance. The *Comet's* doughnut-shaped warp propulsion module would remain in space while its landing craft returned home.

Curt's hands moved across the wraparound control panels, going through the procedure that would separate the torus from the lander. A five-second countdown, then he snapped a set of toggles. A momentary jar, accompanied by a dull clunk, told him that the torus' retractable anchors were disconnected from the lander's sleek hull. Curt fired the maneuvering thrusters and the *Comet* slowly backed out of its warp torus, the tips of its delta wings automatically lowering into flight position, even though they weren't needed for a lunar landing.

Curt waited until the ship was well away from the warp module before he activated the torus' fantome generator. Through the cockpit windows, he watched as the torus faded from sight. It would remain invisible until the rest of the *Comet* returned, and while it was unlikely that another craft in equatorial lunar orbit would come close enough to pose a collision risk, the torus' anti-collision system would detect the other vessel in time to fire the maneuvering thrusters and move the torus away without its presence ever being detected by the other ship.

Again, Curt felt a surge of pride for his craft. Besides the cutters and frigates of the Solar Coalition Navy, the *Comet* was the only vessel to possess an Alcubierre-type warp drive. When President James Carthew decided to commission Curt Newton and his crew as independent agents of the Interplanetary Police Force, he ordered that Curt's original *Comet* – a short-range racing yacht he'd inherited from his late father, destroyed on Mars during his showdown with Ul Quorn and his followers – be replaced with a state-of-the-art space cruiser capable of transporting Captain Future and the Futuremen across the solar system within hours and landing on any planetary surface.

Considered the fastest ship in the solar system, the *Comet* was truly unique. And it was because of this uniqueness that its warp torus had to be protected as an advanced technological asset. The Alcubierre drive was capable of harnessing dark energy and using it to produce a bubble-like field that encompassed the ship and separated it from spacetime, thus allowing it to achieve near-light-speed velocity. Indeed, Simon Wright – Curt's mentor, the cyborg they called the Brain – believed that, with further study and experimentation, such a torus might one day be capable of reaching velocities many times light-speed.

On a nav chart displayed on the cockpit's center screen, a tiny red bullseye strobed just above Tycho Crater, the location of Captain Future's secret base. Curt gradually brought the *Comet* down from orbit; when the ship was within fifty miles of the touchdown point, he kicked in the autopilot and activated the lander's own fantome generator. The cockpit windows immediately went black; the fantome deflected light rays, which meant that the *Comet* would have to take an AI-controlled instrument landing. In a pinch, Simon could take over as pilot, cybernetically connecting himself with the *Comet's* computers, but it wasn't necessary for him to do so this time.

Activating the fantome for landings and liftoffs at Tycho Base was another precaution. Although it was well-known among the public that Captain Future's home base was somewhere on the Moon, its precise location was a closely-guarded secret. Fortunately, Tycho lay in a wilderness region of the Moon's southern hemisphere, so there had never been many people visiting it except the occasional hiking party. The Lunar Republic established Tycho as an off-limits government reserve, banning all visitors from it and claiming the crater contained a high-level nuclear waste site; it even set up a cluster of dummy waste canisters on the crater floor, just in case someone used satellite-imaging to check the cover story. So there was little chance of anyone stumbling on Captain Future's hidden base. Curt considered his secrets to be worth protecting; besides, he didn't want his home to become a tourist attraction.

Therefore, no one was around to see two enormous doors on the crater floor – each carefully camouflaged to resemble the terrain with fake regolith, rocks, and micrometeorite impact craters – bisect and slowly open, revealing the hangar below. As the *Comet* descended on its VTOL thrusters, Curt switched off the fantome as soon as the ship was below the crater walls. By then, the *Comet* no longer needed to be invisible.

The moment he spotted Tycho Base, Curt knew that they had visitors. A lunar hopper was parked near the blasted ruins of the original aboveground base, the one built by Curt's parents but destroyed by Victor Corvo the day he murdered them. The ruins hid the entrance airlock, and Curt recognized the hopper at once as the one used by Lt. Joan Randall, special agent of IPF Section Four.

Shortly after Joan was appointed by IPF Commandant Halk Anders to be the official liaison to Captain Future and the Futuremen, Otho and Grag had taken an ordinary IPF lunar hopper and reprogrammed its transponder to automatically send a signal that, upon approach, would deactivate Tycho Base's defense system. They also fitted the hopper with a fantome generator, enabling the vehicle to become invisible during Joan's sorties to Tycho. Even if the hopper was spotted on the ground by a spacecraft in low orbit, its proximity to the wrecked surface buildings would lead someone to believe that the hopper belonged to someone who was just giving the ruins a look-see.

"Looks like your girlfriend is already here," Otho said drily.

Curt didn't take his eyes off the controls, but nonetheless his face burned. Otho was really getting on his nerves today; he'd been ragging on him ever since they left Venus. "She's not my girlfriend," he muttered

"Oh, yeah, I forgot…the two of you just work together." Although Curt wasn't looking at Otho, he knew there was a sly grin on the android's colorless face. "Is that what you're gonna tell your **old** girlfriend?"

Otho meant Ashi Lanyr, whom Curt had apprehended on Stratos Venera. Ashi and Curt had met and briefly had a romantic affair when they were teenagers; for that reason, Curt had decided to transport her back to the Moon himself, giving him a chance to speak with her and perhaps find out why she'd joined Starry Messenger.

"Shut up about her," Curt said. Already the *Comet's* VTOLs were kicking up fine gray dust from the ground below. "Especially when Joan is around. She doesn't need to know about…about…just keep your mouth shut, okay?"

Otho snickered. He sounded as if he was about to add another wise-ass comment, but restrained himself. Curt was beginning to suspect that, for once, the android was being tactful when another voice spoke up from behind them. "You **are** planning to turn Ma'amoiselle Lanyr over to Joan when we see her, right?"

Simon. He'd come up from below while Curt and Otho were talking. Curt had seen little of his friend and mentor during the return flight from Venus. Because the Brain no longer had a human form – his original body lay buried in a lonesome grave within Tycho Crater, next to those of Roger and Elaine Newton – he occasionally needed to spend time near an electrical outlet, where he could insert the recharger of his modified drone body and recharge its batteries again. And although his cyborg form no longer needed sleep in the human sense, his mind still required several hours of rest every standard day, just as a normal person did. So the Brain had been "asleep" for the entire trip back from Venus, waking up in time for the *Comet's* touchdown at Tycho Base.

Curt didn't reply as he reached down with his left hand, located the lever that operated the *Comet's* tricycle landing gear, and shoved it forward. A faint grind and a solid thump beneath the deck panels told him that the wheels were down. A quick glance through the cockpit; no longer visible were Tycho's rock walls, but instead an oblong pit of burnished lunar steel. The *Comet's* underground hangar, its roof retracted, spotlights reflecting off an elevated landing platform.

A few moments later, there came another thump, this time from the wheels coming to rest upon the hangar's elevator platform. They were home.

VII

As soon as the *Comet* was still, Curt cut the engines. "Extend the catwalk," he said to Otho, "but don't pressurize the hangar. We're not going to be here very long."

"Pluto next?" Simon asked. The impellers on either side of the saucer-like carapace that contained his brain whirred softly as he hovered behind the pilot and co-pilot seats.

"I'd say it's a good bet, but let's hear what Joan and Ezra have to say first." Curt waited until the landing platform began to descend into the underground hangar before he unbuckled the seat harness and carefully rose to his feet. Gravity had returned, and although it was only .2g, that was enough to let them move comfortably about. Curt opened a drawer under his seat, found the two pairs of ankle weights stowed inside, and handed one to Otho before bending down to clip the other about his ankles.

The platform came to rest fifty feet below the crater floor, in a large cavern excavated from lunar rock and fashioned into a spacious hangar. It was created for the original *Comet,* but when the *Comet II* was built, a team of construction 'bots enlarged the hangar to accommodate the larger vessel. It now contained not only the *Comet,* but also several short-range craft, including a lunar hopper, an eight-wheel tandem crawler, and the *Comet's* auxiliary two-seat recon pod.

Spotting the auxiliary pod, Curt made a mental note to swap it for the one-seat pod before they set out for Pluto. As he headed for the flight-deck ladder, there was a dull thud against the *Comet's* hull: the hangar's pressurized gangway, telescoping out to connect with the *Comet's* main airlock.

Curt climbed down to the lower deck, where he found Grag standing guard outside the cabin where Ashi Lanyr was sequestered. "Has she said anything?" Curt asked quietly.

"Not a peep." Grag's oversized head turned to regard Curt with round, red eyes that seemed to be perpetually surprised. "She hasn't even asked why we've landed here and not the IPF post at Descartes City," the robot added as he stepped aside to let Curt approach the cabin.

"Hmm...well, maybe she's figured out that something's come up." Curt started to raise a hand to the door's thumbplate, then stopped himself. *–I'm going to let her out,* he said to Grag, using his Anni to continue his conversation with the 'bot. *–I still want you to stick close to her and not let her out of your sight until I can put her somewhere she won't cause trouble.*

–Understood, chief. Grag's head bobbed up and down. Curt wondered how long the robot had studied a casual gesture most humans took for granted, then learned how and when to imitate it. Becoming human-like was Grag's goal in life. Since he was aware that failure was preordained – try as he might, he'd never become a biological human – he'd decided to not merely emulate *Homo sapiens,* but in fact be better than them. Otho had much the same obsession, and there was a lifelong argument between the two about which of them was better at being superior to humans.

Curt pressed his thumb against the plate. A soft click and a winking green light told him that he could now open the door. He slid it aside an inch or so. "Hello, are you decent?"

"My, aren't we chivalrous?" A quiet laugh. "Yes, I'm decent...please come in."

"Thank you." Curt slid the door the rest of the way open and walked in.

Ashi was fully clothed, still wearing the skintight bodysuit customarily worn beneath pressure gear. She stood at the cabin porthole gazing out at the underground hangar, and when she turned to Curt, she had the sort of smile that, not long ago, was guaranteed to turn his knees to butter.

To Curt's surprise, it still did. If he thought he was no longer attracted to her, he was wrong. And that was dangerous.

"Obviously we haven't rendezvoused with an IPF ship or landed at Descartes City," she said.

"No," Curt replied. "A little change of plans."

"Uh-huh." She idly tapped a fingertip against the cabin porthole. "Tycho...that's where we've landed, yes? Tycho Crater."

Surprised, Curt raised an eyebrow. It should have been difficult, if not impossible, for Ashi to know for certain where they were. Since the fantome field rendered the porthole opaque, she wouldn't have been able to recognize Tycho during the *Comet's* primary approach and descent. And although the field was turned off during the ship's final descent, by then the *Comet* was below the crater walls. From low altitude, it would've been difficult to distinguish Tycho from any of the Moon's other large impact craters. Yet, she'd surmised this so accurately, Curt knew it was no wild guess.

"How do you know that?" he asked.

"Oh, c'mon." Ashi's smile become mildly mocking. "You really think Starry Messenger **doesn't** know where you live?"

Curt stared at her. "What else do they know about me?" he asked, trying not to appear as stunned as he felt.

"Oh no, you don't." The young woman he'd apprehended as a terrorist shook her head. "You're not getting anything from me so easily, even if you were once my boyfriend. I hope IPF interrogators are better at prying secrets out of people than you are." Before Curt could reply, she stepped away from the porthole. "Well, okay...you've brought me home, so why don't you fix me a drink and show me around?"

"Damn, you **are** brazen, aren't you?" Laughing, Curt beckoned to the door. "I wouldn't count on that drink...the only person here who enjoys that particular vice is Otho, and I doubt that he'll let you visit his wine closet. But I might let you see a little of the place before IPF comes to haul you away."

"Okay. Fine." Ashi started to step past him, then stopped. "You're not going to put me in cuffs, are you?"

Curt didn't respond. He didn't usually bring scofflaws to Tycho Base, so unlike IPF stations, there were few provisions for holding prisoners here, handcuffs included. At least that was one thing about Tycho that Starry Messenger apparently didn't know. "Depends. If you're going to give us any trouble –"

"I won't." She raised a hand, palm out. "While I'm here, you have my word that I'll behave myself. I won't try to escape. That I promise."

Curt was glad Otho wasn't around; he would've laughed out loud to hear this. But knowing Ashi as he did, Curt also knew that she could be trusted not to break a promise. "All right," he said, "I'll hold you to your word." He turned to the door. "Don't make me sorry that I did," he added as they left the cabin. Ashi didn't reply except for a brief nod.

By then, Otho had finished shutting down the *Comet* and had descended from the flight deck as well, Simon floating down right behind him. Ashi paid little attention to Otho – like most people, she apparently mistook him for a selenite, not realizing that his snow-white skin and hairless head weren't the racial characteristics of *Homo cosmos luna* – but recoiled from Simon, as many people did when they met the Brain for the first time. Simon had long become accustomed to this reaction, though, and learned to take advantage of it.

"Mademoiselle Lanyr," he said formally, "if you'll please come with me, I'll escort you to our living quarters." Impellers whirring, Simon floated toward her, manipulator claws making the same sort of polite gestures that people would with their hands. Ashi shrank back even further, and Curt had to cover his mouth to keep from laughing. The Brain loved freaking out people this way…

The pressurized gangway had been extended to mate with the *Comet*. It led across the airless cavern to the base's primary airlock. Since they were coming off the ship without first putting on pressure gear and stepping out onto the lunar surface, there was no need to walk through regolith scrubbers to remove the abrasive dust that was the bane of everyday life on the Moon. Once everyone had disembarked, Curt sealed the *Comet's* main hatch. At the other end of the gangway, as he approached the airlock to turn its lockwheel, he glanced back at Grag, who was standing behind him and Ashi.

"We're probably not going to be here very long," he said to the 'bot, "so I want you to start prepping the *Comet* for the next mission. Refuel the VTOLs and swap out the one-seat pod for the two-seater. We'll need the extreme-environment surface gear, too, so go into the suit locker and get –"

Curt was cut short by the dull snap of the hatch being undogged from the other side. It swung open, revealing a young woman, tall and athletically slender, with dark brown hair cut to neck-length, but with long bangs touching her eyebrows. She wore the dark blue jumpsuit of an IPF officer, the silver bars on her shoulder epaulets attesting to her rank as lieutenant.

"Welcome back," Joan Randall said, none too warmly. Her voice was even, but her blue eyes flared with anger barely suppressed. "I got Simon's mission report and read it. Damn it, Curt, what do you think you're doing, taking risks like that?"

"Hi, Joan. Miss me?" Curt kept the smile on his face, but inwardly he winced. Simon Wright wrote a report of each mission as soon as it'd been completed, which was immediately submitted to the IPF as a matter of routine. In her role as the Futuremen's IPF liaison, Joan reviewed these reports as soon as Simon sent them; if she hadn't accompanied Captain Future and the Futuremen on their latest mission for the IPF, this was how she learned what had happened while they were on assignment.

The Brain's reports were usually straight-forward accounts, with little or no embellishment. Nonetheless, they occasionally included details that Curt wished Simon had left out. In this instance, he guessed that Joan must have read the part where Curt had jumped from the recon pod to Venera Stratos's rotorvator while it was in the descent mode of its passage through Venus' upper stratosphere, miles above the cloud layer that permanently hid the planet's surface from sight. It hadn't been a particularly long jump – an Earth child could have done it easily in his or her school playground – nevertheless, it would have been a fatal error if Curt had somehow missed and plummeted into Venus's lethal atmosphere, and Joan…

Joan's relationship with Curt had become rather complicated lately.

Over the past several years, the two of them had become steadily infatuated with each other. Captain Future wasn't supposed to have a romantic affair with his IPF liaison, though, so he and Joan had tried to maintain a line between duty and personal life. For a while, they'd managed to resist their mutual attraction, but the affair had happened nonetheless, and there wasn't much they could do about it. They hid it as best they could, and although the Futuremen couldn't help but notice that Lt. Randall slept in Curt's room when she visited Tycho, they did their best to make sure that her superiors were unaware of this...most especially Ezra Gurney, Joan's boss in IPF Section Four.

But a relationship is a difficult thing to maintain if one person is constantly putting his life in mortal danger. Like jumping from a spacecraft hatch to a moving rotarvator with nothing below except acid-laden clouds that would've stripped his body to the bones before he even reached the ground.

"Of all the reckless, irresponsible, **stupid** things to do –" Joan began.

"Thanks," Curt said, grinning at her anger. "Nice to see you, too."

Joan seemed to realize that scolding Curt was pointless, because she closed her eyes and let out her breath. "Yeah, well...welcome home," she finished, stepping aside to let him pass.

More than anything, Curt wanted to put his arms around her and greet her with a nice, long kiss. But that couldn't be done, not with others around...and especially not in the presence of the tall, gray-haired man standing just outside the airlock in the adjacent ready-room.

"Welcome home, son." Ezra Gurney, IPF marshal and Section 4 chief, waited for Curt to pass through the airlock into the ready-room before offering a handshake. His voice had the slow, lazy accent of a loonie, his smile all but hidden beneath his salt-and-pepper handlebar mustache. "Glad to hear the mission was a success. Is that the perp y'all arrested?"

He meant Ashi, who'd come in behind Curt. "This is her, yes," Curt said, and shook his head when Gurney reached for the magnetic handcuffs dangling from his uniform belt. "Ma'amoiselle Lanyr has given her word that she won't give us any trouble if we don't put the cuffs on her. And I think she may have something to offer us."

"I kinda doubt that." Eyes narrowing to an inquisitive squint, Ezra regarded Ashi as if she was a rodent who'd stowed away aboard the *Comet* and he'd found sneaking in through the airlock.

"Marshal Gurney...you **are** Marshal Gurney, aren't you?" Ashi asked, and Ezra nodded, surprised to be recognized by a terror suspect. "I think I'm right to assume that the reason why I've been brought here and not to Descartes City is that something's come up that has something to do with Starry Messenger." She looked at Curt. "Is that right? Is that why I'm here?"

Curt hesitated, then nodded. Ezra didn't respond at once, though, but continued to study Ashi, weighing her words. He wasn't the only one suspicious of her. "That's really none of your –" Joan began.

"Let's hear what she has to say," Curt interrupted. "Then we'll decide what needs to be done." He turned to Grag again. "Go do the things I asked you to do, please. Link up with my Anni so you can listen in." He then looked at the others. "Let's go to the main room. We'll begin by you briefing us on what's going on, starting with the *Titan King*."

VIII

Tycho Base's underground lair consisted of a circular main room thirty feet in diameter, with smaller, wedge-shaped rooms branching off from it like pie cuts. Most of the smaller rooms were living space – bedrooms, bathrooms and adjacent spa, kitchens, storerooms, hydroponic greenhouse – but several were labs put together by Roger Newton for the work that he, Elaine, and Simon Wright had come to the Moon to do, before murder and destruction arrived in the form of Victor Corvo.

Over the years, Curt and his companions had gradually altered this place, the only home he'd ever known, as necessity dictated. Yet there was one thing that remained the same: the main room.

The room had a dome ceiling twelve feet above the floor. At its apex was a light shaft leading up to a circular atrium window, its airtight lunaglass several inches thick. Like the *Comet's* hangar, the window was concealed by camouflaged shutters fashioned to resemble the surrounding lunar terrain. When uncovered, the atrium helped illuminate the room: sunlight during the two-week lunar day, earthlight during the equally long lunar night.

Directly beneath the light shaft was one of the base's few permanent fixtures, a long worktable carved from a slab of lunar basalt. Although polished to a fine finish, over time its surface had been discolored and pitted by hard use. Fashioned by Grag himself, when he'd been merely one of the construction 'bots who built Tycho Base, the table had been there from the very first day Roger Newton arrived with his family. Surrounded by faux-leather armchairs, it served as everything from dining table to lab bench.

Now the table served as the stage for miniature drama: a holographic message from the Black Pirate, the man who'd hijacked the *Titan King* three months ago and was now responsible for the prison uprising on Pluto.

A doll-sized image of the pirate chief was projected on the table. He was seated in what appeared to be a spacecraft control room, probably the *Titan King*'s bridge. Legs crossed, hands comfortably resting at his sides, the Black Pirate was relaxed and sure of himself, yet there was something about the way his eyes gleamed within his mask. The red lenses caught and reflected the light from overhead panels, making his eyes shine like those of a nocturnal predator. A wolf in space.

"We received this just a little while ago, while you were still on Stratos Venera." Ezra Gurney was seated at the opposite end of the table from Curt. Otho, Simon, and Joan were there was well, as was Ashi Lanyr, her good behavior assured by the police collar the marshal had fastened around her neck almost as soon as she came off the *Comet*.

"It was transmitted via laser to Farside," Ezra went on, "but we think it was really meant for…well, maybe you oughta hear this yourself."

He touched his wristband and the holo became animated. "Greetings," the Black Pirate said. His voice was altered, an electronic purr lacking any accent or inflection that might help identify him. "My name is unimportant. What matters more is what I have to tell you –"

"Sure thing, pal," Otho muttered, "but I still wanna know who the hell you are."

"Shh!" Curt hissed. "I want to hear this."

"A few months ago," the Black Pirate continued, "my comrades and I seized control of the *Titan King,* which we've subsequently rechristened the *Liberator.* When we did this, I made the decision to release all of the passengers and most of the crew –"

"Yeah, you're a real humanitarian," Otho grumbled. Curt shot him a look and he raised his hands: *okay, I'll shut up.*

"Of the latter," the Black Pirate was saying, "nearly all who stayed did so as individuals who've elected to join our cause. The only person kept as a hostage was the *King's* former commanding officer, Captain Henri Lamont."

He made a small hand gesture; a second later Captain Lamont suddenly appeared beside him, staggering slightly as if he'd been pushed into camera range. Lamont still wore his uniform; he appeared to be harried but unhurt, a man who'd been treated reasonably well and yet – the defiant look in his eyes attested to this – had refused to cooperate with his captors

"I'm Lamont," he said, standing at stiff attention beside the chair he'd once occupied, "and I can vouch for what this man has said. I have not been physically harmed, and I'm the only remaining member of the *Titan King's* crew –" he cast an angry glare at someone off-screen "– who hasn't thrown in with these goddamn –"

"Language, Captain…language." The Black Pirate's tone was mocking. Another flick of his wrist, and Lamont was abruptly jerked away by a pair of hands that appeared and disappeared again. The pirate's red eyes followed him. "After all I've done to assure the safety of your crew and passengers," he complained, shaking his head, "and this is the gratitude I get!"

"Yeah, what a nice guy." Now it was Ezra's turn. The old marshal looked as if he wanted to reach into the holo and wrap his hands around the buccaneer's throat.

"The same treatment is being afforded to a certain individual who is currently incarcerated here," the Black Pirate went on. "Although most of the inmates will be released, this individual will continue to be held hostage along with Captain Lamont. The lives of both men will be forfeited unless my demands are met."

"Here it comes," Joan said softly.

"First, we demand one hundred million dollars SolCol," the pirate leader said, citing the form of electronic currency used through the Solar Coalition. "This money will be deposited in an account that will be revealed to you once your representative has arrived on Pluto. This individual, whom we'll name in just a moment, will come to Cold Hell, where he will be admitted once we've been assured that he is unarmed. He will bring with him a credit chit from the Bank of the Lunar Republic for the stated amount…and the chit had better be clean of any viruses, watermarks, or encryptions, because we'll be checking to make sure. Once we've ascertained that that it's a clean chit, the one hundred million will be transferred to an account in a financial institution elsewhere in the system."

Curt raised a hand, and Ezra touched his wristband again. "Isn't there a way of tracing the ransom once this transfer has been made?"

"Not if they scan the card," Ezra said, "and it sounds like they will." He shook his head. "I'm betting the second account is for a bank on Mars, but in any case, I ain't inclined to play games with these characters…not if they're holding a gun to Lamont's head."

"There is also the other prisoner to consider," Simon said. He hovered at the table beside Curt, his eyestalks making slight movements as he looked first at the holo, then Ezra, then the holo again. "That individual may be a convict, but we have to take our friend here at his word that he'll kill his hostages if his demands aren't satisfied."

"Agreed," Curt said, "but let's hear the rest of this, okay?" He looked over at Ezra; the marshal nodded quietly and resumed the playback.

"At this time," the Black Pirate continued, "Captain Lamont and our other hostage will be released to you, and shortly after that, the *Liberator* will depart. With the exception of a few we'll be taking with us, our comrades from Starry Messenger who've been imprisoned here, the inmates will remain where we found them. However —" a brief pause "— I regret to inform you that Warden Jeerdin and all the prison's guards and staff members were liquidated by sentry 'bots when we took control of them. These casualties couldn't be helped, and I apologize for the necessity of our actions."

"Necessity?" Curt shot to his feet, snarling at the Black Pirate as if he was in the same room. "You barbarian! You didn't need to —"

"You're right," Ezra said, freezing the image again. "'Barbarian' pretty much describes this rat bastard."

"As soon as we received this," Joan quietly added, "Section Four accessed the real-time telemetry of the medical implants worn by everyone in Cold Hell, staff and prisoners alike. The situation is as he says it is…everyone on the prison staff, from Warden Jeerdin on down, is dead, while all the prisoners are still alive."

"So much for pretendin' to be merciful," Ezra drawled, "this guy is a stone killer." Ezra touched his wristband again. "Here comes the interestin' part …"

"We have a major stipulation." As the Black Pirate spoke, he stood up from his chair. Now they could see him from head to toe, a tall and ominous figure, formidable even as a miniature holo projection. "The person we want to deliver the ransom to us is Curt Newton, otherwise known as Captain Future."

"He knows your name!" Otho exclaimed. "How the hell does he —?"

"Quiet." Curt held up a hand. "I want to hear the rest of this."

"Captain Future," the Black Pirate went on, "if you're watching this...and I have little doubt that you are...your instructions are as follows. You are to land your vessel, the *Comet*, on the prison's landing field, in an area that will be marked with your initials, CF. You, along with everyone else aboard, will then disembark and proceed on foot to the prison's main gate. None of you will carry any arms, and the *Comet's* guns and other armaments will remain in their stowed positions. Your party will stay outside while you alone will come in."

"I don't like that," Joan said quietly.

"Neither do I," Curt replied, but it went without saying that they weren't being given a choice.

"Once you've gone through the airlock," the Black Pirate continued, "you will hand over the credit chit to the person who will meet you there. After the funds have been transferred and we're confident that you've done nothing to betray us, Captain Lamont and our other hostage will be released and the three of you will be allowed to leave. You and your party will then return to the *Comet*. Your ship will lift off from the prison, and once we're sure that you've left Pluto and are on your way home, the *Liberator* will depart as well."

As he spoke, the Black Pirate strolled away from the command chair. The camera followed him, and as the pirate walked across the control room, Captain Lamont came back into view. He was seated at a bridge station, hands folded together helplessly. A large jovian stood behind him, his enormous hands resting on Lamont's shoulders; Curt wondered if this was the *Titan King's* helmsman, said to be among the liner's bridge officers to throw in with the pirates. Harl al-Sarakka, his face and bio now on IPF's Most Wanted list.

"I'll give you twenty-four hours to get here, M'sieur Newton...or Captain Future, if you prefer," the Black Pirate said. "The *Comet* is capable of reaching Pluto in that short amount of time, so this is not an extraordinary demand. If I don't see your face by this hour tomorrow Standard Solar Time, we'll execute our hostages, one by one. And while Captain Lamont may be considered expendable, we both know President Carthew won't sacrifice the life of even a convicted criminal."

While he spoke, the Black Pirate's right hand drifted within the folds of his cape. It reappeared, this time holding a particle-beam pistol. With almost casual disdain, he moved its barrel until it was almost resting against Lamont's temple. The liner captain flinched but said nothing; there was no point in pretending that the gun wasn't there.

"The *Comet* is said to be the fastest ship in the system," the Black Pirate finished. "Let's see if that's true. Twenty-four hours, Newton, or I'll pull the trigger on him. And we'll hand his body over to the kuiperians...they may enjoy some fresh meat."

He lowered his PBP and stepped away from Lamont. "Captain Future, the matter is now in your hands. Choose wisely."

The communique ended abruptly, the holo image becoming a phosphorescent cloud that quickly dissipated. Ezra Gurney let out his breath and turned to Curt.

"There it is," he said. "And by the way, you don't have twenty-four hours to get to Pluto any more...it's more like twenty now."

"Plenty of time." The Brain moved forward to hover closer to the place where the holo had been. "I just linked with the *Comet's* navigation system and calculated a fastest-route flight plan. If we leave within an hour, we can reach Pluto in ten hours and twenty-two minutes, with a fifteen minute margin of error."

"Excellent. Thanks, Simon." Curt absently drummed his fingers upon the tabletop. "Now we just have to figure out a rescue plan for –"

"No, Curt." Joan shook her head. "I'm sorry, but there won't be a rescue attempt."

Curt stared at her. "What? Why?"

"Commandant Anders has ordered us to comply with the Black Pirate's demands. Any attempt to rescue Lamont will put his life and the other hostage at risk."

"If we find Lamont," Otho said, "we can save him, no problem. But as for the other guy –" he snorted and shook his head "– we don't know who that is, but may I remind you that some of the worst people in the system are incarcerated in Cold Hell? Ezra, how many of 'em are guys we put there ourselves?"

"Too many to count," Ezra replied. "I don't know why he didn't name the other one, but I'm guessin' that guy is the pirates' trump card, to be played if we decide that Lamont can be sacrificed."

"He's got a point," Curt said to Otho. "There are some bad people on Pluto. Grey Garson, Xov Yad and Gert Noes, Larsen King –"

"Not to mention our favorite scumbag," Otho added quietly.

Curt nodded. No one there needed to be reminded of his name...almost no one. "Who are you talking about?" Ashi Lanyr asked, speaking up for the first time since entering Tycho Base.

"Victor Corvo," Joan replied. "That is, **Senator** Victor Corvo." She looked at Curt as she said this, emphasizing the fact that the man who'd killed Roger and Elaine Newton was also the former Senator of the Lunar Republic.

"I'm afraid she's right, lad," the Brain said. "There would be a heavy price to pay if we allowed Corvo to be killed, even though he may deserve it. As a former Senate member, the political repercussions of his death would be high."

"Even if he's traitor?" Curt asked.

"Yes, I'm afraid so. After all, his treason conviction is still disputed by some."

Curt quietly nodded. The Brain was right. During Victor Corvo's impeachment hearing, which removed him from the Solar Coalition Senate, and his subsequent criminal trial by the Superior Court of the Lunar Republic, his lawyers had tried to claim that all the charges against the Senator had been fabricated by President Carthew. Testimony by Curt – as Captain Future – and Joan had persuaded both the Senate and the Superior Court jury that Corvo was indeed responsible for high crimes and misdemeanors, not the least of which were the murders of Roger and Elaine Newton. Yet to this day, there were some who believed in the ridiculous political conspiracy that Carthew had framed Corvo in order to get a political opponent out of the way.

"That's why Halk Anders is under orders of his own," Joan said. "And they come straight from the top...the top floor of Government Tower, that is."

Curt bit his lip. There was but one occupant of the highest floor of Government Tower in New York, and James Carthew's authority as President of the Solar Coalition was absolute. When he said no chances were to be taken with the lives of Captain Lamont or Cold Hell's residents, that was final.

Curt had picked up an old slang expression from a lifetime hobby of watching twentieth century vids (or as they were called then, "movies"). "So I'm just supposed to be a bag man," he said.

He was expecting the Brain to respond. Simon Wright's mind, permanently linked to Anni's limitless resources, could define even an obscure phrase like that in less than a second. Instead, it was Joan Randall who understood, although that shouldn't be surprising given the number of times that she and Curt had curled up to watch those old vids together.

"If you think all you have to do is deliver the ransom," Joan said, "then think again. There's more to this than we can tell you just now."

"What –?"

"Later, Curt," Ezra said. "Soon as we're outta here and on our way, we'll tell you in private."

As the old marshal addressed him verbally, Curt heard Ezra's sub-audible voice in his mind, carried there by their Anni link.

–There's classified info that Joan and I need to share with you and your crew that we can't talk about while Lanyr can hear us. But she's coming with us, so it'll have to wait until the Comet *is in warp so she can't use her Anni to tell someone on the outside.*

Surprised, Curt almost replied verbally. But he remembered to answer the same way so only Ezra could hear him.

–You want to bring Ashi? Why?

–She may be useful. Leave it to me, boy. I've got an excuse all nice 'n ready.

Ezra gave him a wink as he said this. Curt pretended not to notice. "Okay, then I guess that covers about everything," he said, pushing back his chair and standing up. "We better hurry up and get packed. Otho, I want us ready to lift off within the hour…think you can help Grag get the *Comet* ready by then?"

"No sweat, chief." Otho cocked his head toward Ashi. "What about her? Aren't we going to hand her over to the IPF?"

"We're –" Ezra began.

"I wouldn't do that if I were you." Ashi Lanyr had spoken little since arriving on the Moon. She spoke up now. "I belonged to Starry Messenger, remember?"

"'Belonged'?" Joan's mouth curled at Ashi's use of the past tense. "When did you quit, five minutes ago?"

Ashi ignored her; she directed her comments to Curt and Ezra. "You don't know who the Black Pirate is, do you?" Curt reluctantly shook his head; Ezra said nothing, but let his fingers play with the tips of his mustache. "Well, I do. In fact, I'm one of the few people who's seen him without his mask. And I'll tell you who he is and why he's taken over Cold Hell, but –"

"But only if we don't hand you over to the IPF but let you tag along instead." Ezra let out his breath as a disgusted sigh. "Lady, it's people like you who really piss me off…no loyalty, not even to the folks who took you in."

"Nobody 'took me in'!" Ashi snapped, dark eyes blazing as they swung toward the old lawman.

"Not according to your IPF dossier," Joan murmured. "Bet you didn't even know you had one, did you?"

"Who's the Black Pirate?" Curt didn't care about the reasons why Ashi was coming with them. All he wanted to know was the identity of the man behind the mask. "Tell us now, Ashi."

She shook her head. "No...not until we're on the way to Pluto."

Curt glanced at Ezra. The marshal nodded but didn't say anything to him, either with his tongue or through his neural-net link. "Very well, then," Curt said reluctantly. "You're coming along...but as a prisoner, and a suspected terrorist at that."

Otho looked like he was going to object. Curt noticed the android's change of expression. "You'll be confined to quarters except when you're needed," he added, "and Grag will be assigned to guard you until we're home again. Any trouble from you, we might just skip the formalities of a jury trial and have President Carthew issue an executive order for us to leave you in Cold Hell. Understood?"

Ashi's face paled. She looked down at the table, nodding ever so slightly. "Very well, then," Curt finished. "Otho, come help me check out the EE suits before Grag loads them. Joan, go to the armory and pick out the guns we'll need. No ballistic firearms, remember, just energy weapons...they're the only things that won't jam in the cold. Simon, I need you in the *Comet* to help me run through the checklist. Everyone know their assignments? All right, let's go."

Everyone left the table and went their separate ways. All except Ezra, who was slow to leave. He lingered near Ashi, ready to lead her over to the base's small holding cell where she would remain until the *Comet* was ready to depart. He caught Curt's eye and strolled over to him, leaving Ashi alone but not out of sight.

"Is that the excuse you were going to use?" Curt murmured, turning his back to her.

"No," Ezra whispered back. "I had something else in mind. Didn't have a clue she was goin' to say what she did."

Curt gave him a sharp look. "So you don't know who the Black Pirate is either?"

"We **think** we do…but that's something else I'm gonna keep to myself until we're out of here." Ezra hesitated. "You're not gonna like it, kid…warning you now, it's going to be something you don't wanna hear."

Before Curt could ask more, Ezra turned and walked back to where he'd left Ashi.

IX

When Victor Corvo heard people screaming outside his cell, his first reaction was annoyance at the interruption of a quiet morning.

Over the past five standard years, the former Senator of the Lunar Republic had adjusted to prison life by adopting a daily routine that offered comfort in predictability. He woke up, used the toilet, bathed, got dressed, went to the mess hall for breakfast, reported to his job in the laundry room, had lunch, then spent the afternoon as a gentleman of leisure: strolling around the courtyard, reading in the library, or playing chess, bridge, or tourney with other inmates. After dinner, he'd return to his cell, lay on his bunk and watch a vid or read until lights-out. A dull life far removed from the luxuries he'd once enjoyed, but it was all he had left so he sought to make the best of it.

When Corvo heard Aux and Bobbi, the two human guards who worked the morning shift in Cell Block 21, start shouting at someone or something, he was on his bunk putting on his mocs. He looked up, more irritated than alarmed. Another fight. He almost yelled for them to knock it off when angry shouts suddenly changed to terrified screams; that was when he realized that what was happening elsewhere in his cell block was more serious than a fistfight or even someone getting shivved.

While in the Senate, Corvo usually brought IPF bodyguards with him when he went out in public; Starry Messenger often made threats against Senate members who didn't support Martian and outer-system independence. No one knew that Corvo was secretly backing the separatists, so it was unlikely that he'd become one of their targets; his escorts were there for show, really. While rehearsing emergency procedures, his IPF handlers had taught him that, at the first sign of trouble, he was to take cover, keep quiet, and wait for the all-clear.

That's what Corvo did now. His cell, which he didn't share with anyone, was small and windowless, with a bunk that folded out from the wall, a small desk, and a chair. The bunk was too narrow to hide beneath, but the desk had a leg-well with just enough room for him to crawl into and not be seen.

Almost. Over the past several years, starchy prison food and lack of strenuous exercise had caused Corvo to loose the good looks he'd once enjoyed. He was overweight and chunky now, with hair that was gray and thinning, and a distinct roll of fat under his chin. Crunching his legs against his chest was difficult, but the former senator managed to squeeze his body beneath the desk. There he played possum – an old looney expression; what the hell was a possum, anyway? – and waited for someone to come along and restore order.

Inmate riots were rare in Cold Hell but not unheard of, so that's what he thought was going on. Inevitably, it would be suppressed, and since he didn't want to lose his privileges – and really, when it came right down to it, he was a coward – he'd long since decided that the best policy was to keep his head down and refrain from joining the riot. Not for an instant did Victor Corvo suspect that a breakout was in progress; they were even more rare than riots. Who'd want to escape from a prison if doing so meant freezing to death, being devoured by cannibals, or both?

He was still under the desk, hearing little but the eerie silence that had fallen across the prison, when a voice came from above his bunk.

"Hello…hello, can anyone hear me?"

Corvo cautiously peered out from under the desk. The wallscreen above his bunk had come to life. It showed a figure in black, face hidden by a mask, standing in stikshoes before a large wraparound porthole, the kind commonly seen in a ship's command center.

"Hi there," said the figure. His voice was electronically distorted, but nonetheless there was a pleasant informality to it. "We've never met before, so just call me the Black Pirate. If you're watching or hearing this, then it's safe to assume that you've survived…well, let's call it an aggressive change in prison management."

A dry chuckle. "Seriously, in case you haven't noticed, the prison staff has been eliminated. Everyone from the warden down, including the guards, have been executed. The sentry 'bots we reprogrammed to do this were instructed to not target anyone their transponder identified as being an inmate. So if you're still breathing, that means you're either an inmate who's just been freed or you're a screw the 'bots haven't located yet. And if it's the latter –" another chuckle "–then run, you bastard. **Run!**"

By now, Victor had crawled out from under the desk. The first thing he did was check his cell door. It was unlocked and open. Quietly as he could, he stepped out. All around Cell Block 21, on all three levels overlooking its small commons, other inmates were doing the same, like shy hermits coming out of hiding. Everyone saw the same thing: their guards, Takka Aux and Bobbi Schwartz, an aresian and a terran respectively, lay dead in the commons, their bodies sharing a pool of blood. A sentry 'bot stood motionless above them, particle beam rifle pointed at the ceiling. Its amber eyes swiveled from one prisoner to the next, but the 'bot didn't demand that anyone to return to their cell.

The Black Pirate continued to speak, his voice reverberating from other wallscreens around the cell block. "My comrades and I belong to Starry Messenger. We're aboard the *Liberator*, a kronite spaceliner we've recently hijacked. Your freedom is the next phase of a plan to bring political independence to the worlds of the outer system. Some of you are political prisoners and some aren't, but we'll hope that all of you will join us in this great effort. If you don't wish to do so, then you need do nothing but step aside and not interfere. Either way, your cooperation will be appreciated, and your participation will be rewarded."

Corvo looked around the cell block. Standing in the open doors of their cells, other inmates glanced at one another as they listened to the Black Pirate. A couple of guys on his third-floor row, Gray Garson and Athor Az, looked back at him, apparently waiting to see how he reacted. Garson and Athor remembered when Victor

Corvo was a senator; they might be criminals, but they were criminals who voted since, for better or worse, the Solar Coalition allowed convicts to participate in elections. Because of that, they were among those in Cold Hell who often looked to him for leadership. Corvo nodded to the terran and the aphrodite and they nodded back.

"The crew of the *Liberator* will be there soon," the Black Pirate continued. "Once we've arrived, we will meet with anyone who wants to volunteer for this great cause. Those we choose will be told the rest of the plan. Those not selected or who decide not to join us –" a brief pause "– will be allowed to leave Pluto in peace aboard whatever vessels they find on the landing field."

The pause was just long enough to make Corvo wonder if the Black Pirate meant to keep his word. If so, then being told that their alternative to joining Starry Messenger was stealing a prison spacecraft wasn't much of a choice. Even if you were able to pilot a ship – Corvo had, but he was only one of a handful of prisoners who could – then where could you go? Pluto was the only inhabited minor planet in the Kuiper Belt, and the nearest colonies, the kronian satellites of Saturn, were months away, depending on Saturn's current position in relation to Pluto. So aside from staying put and meekly waiting for the IPF to show up and retake control of the prison, their only option was joining the pirates.

Corvo had a vision of himself wearing a bandana around his head and a patch over one eye, cutlass in hand and a parrot perched on his shoulder. He was still grinning about this when the Black Pirate finished his little speech. "In any case, we are looking forward to seeing you soon. You can expect our arrival within the hour. So we hope to –"

He abruptly stopped as if recalling something. "Oh, yes…one more thing. As I understand, Senator Victor Corvo is among you. Senator, if you hear me, please come to the monitor room after our shuttle lands. I would particularly like to see you."

Then the screen went blank.

X

An hour later, a group of inmates used a dead guard's all-access keycard to let themselves into the monitor room. Among them was the former Senator of the Lunar Republic.

Corvo stood out among the other prisoners, not only because he alone hadn't picked up any of the guards' particle-beam rifles and pistols, but also the dignified way he carried himself. Corvo had always been a criminal, but he'd never been a lowlife. Even here in Cold Hell, he was called Senator by inmates and guards alike. The title just seemed to fit him, although now it was little more than a prison nickname.

So it was only to be expected that Corvo would assume a leadership role among the newly-freed inmates. Over the past hour, he'd organized them as best he could, starting with the men from his own cell block. Gray Garson and Athor Az became his right-hand men, so they were among the inmates who'd come with Corvo to greet the Black Pirate.

Shortly after they reached the monitor room, the shuttle from the *Liberator* touched down on the landing field. The shuttle was designed to carry tourists on sightseeing excursions among Saturn's moons, so there was enough room to transport nearly all the pirates down to Pluto's surface. A pressurized ice crawler was waiting for them. Mounted high on heated wire-mesh wheels, its chassis mated directly with the shuttle's main airlock, allowing passengers to be carried straight to the prison without first having to don bulky EE suits. Once it was fully loaded, the ice crawler withdrew its pressurized gangway, then drove past the field's control tower and the row of crucified skeletons to Cold Hell's main entrance.

The outer gates opened and the crawler entered the vehicle airlock, where it stood for a few minutes while the chamber was sealed and pressurized. The inner gates then parted and the ice crawler drove the rest of the way into the prison, where it came to a halt within an enclosed exercise yard. The yard was crowded; nearly all of Cold Hell's residents had come to greet their liberators.

The men and women who came off the shuttle were scowling, heavily-armed cutthroats. Besides terrans and selenites, there were also aresians, kronites, and jovians, all inhabitants of the solar system's outer worlds. Some had been the *Titan King*'s hijackers; others were former members of the liner's crew who'd adopted Starry Messenger's cause as their own.

Their leader was the last to disembark.

The Black Pirate walked into the toughest prison in the solar system like he owned the place. Surrounded by his crew, he marched through the yard, acknowledging the cheers of the liberated prisoners with an upraised hand. At this moment, if he'd told them to put on EE suits, leave the prison, and proceed on foot to the kuiperian settlement of Bernard's Landing and slaughter every man, woman, and child they found, they would've done so without hesitation or question. He was now their leader.

Immediately, the inmates found someone to lead the Black Pirate and a couple of his men to the monitor room, where they knew the warden had been when the prison's sentry 'bots opened fire on the guards and other staff members. The Black Pirate took a keycard off the body of a murdered guard, then he and his followers used it to open doors in the prison's subsurface maze until, using an elevator to reach the top deck of the central tower, they reached the monitor room.

Casually stepping over the bodies of Edward Jeerdin and Omar bin-Nerrivik, the Black Pirate paused to examine the room. Like every other place they'd seen so far in Cold Hell, it smelled of death. The murdered warden and the jovian guard lay sprawled face down amid scattered chess pieces; it appeared that they'd been in the middle of a game. The Black Pirate absently nudged the white king with the toe of his black boot and smiled.

"Checkmate," he said softly. He then looked up and seemed to notice Victor Corvo for the first time "Greetings, Senator. Many thanks for helping us secure the facilities."

"You're welcome." Despite appearances, Corvo was intimidated by the man who stood before him. The Black Pirate towered above the former senator, a muscular figure in black, the scarlet lining of his cape matching the color of his eyes. Corvo suddenly became self-conscious of his own appearance, the way he'd let things slide over the past few years. He sucked in his gut and squared his shoulders as he stepped forward to offer his hand.

"I'm the one who's grateful, m'sieur…um …" He waited for the Black Pirate to introduce himself. He didn't, nor did he shake Corvo's hand. "Well, anyway, it's good to see you here. We all appreciate what you've –"

"Seize him."

At the Black Pirate's command, two of his men, an aresian and a jovian, quickly came forward. Before he or any of the other inmates could react, they took Corvo by the arms, bracing him between them. Some of the inmates yelled and started to raise their weapons, but they weren't fast enough. The pirates were ready and had them covered in a second.

"What the hell is this?" Corvo tried to yank loose from the men holding him by the arms, but they held tight. "I thought you were here to free us!"

"We're here to free **them**." Although distorted by the mask's vocalizer, the Black Pirate's voice was pleasant. "You, on the other hand, are not to be trusted. I'd consider having you stripped naked and thrown outside were it not for the fact that I have use for you."

"What do you think you're –?"

"Shut up." The Black Pirate was no longer easy-going, and his command was enough to silence Corvo. Once he'd gone quiet, the pirate leader looked at the men holding him. "One more word out of Senator Corvo –" his voice was frosted with sarcasm "– and you're to shoot him in the head."

A stringy-haired man to Corvo's left silently placed the muzzle of his PBP against the former senator's temple. Corvo's eyes widened, but he didn't say a word.

"What are you doing?" Gray Garson stared at the pirate chief. "The Senator is –"

"Garson, isn't it?" The Black Pirate turned to him. "Gray Garson, the former industrialist? The one who got sent up for trying to sabotage his competitors?"

"That's me." A handsome young man whose thick dark hair had become prematurely gray – hence the nickname – Garson nodded. A smile playing at the corners of his mouth; he was flattered to be recognized, even by another criminal. "I still want to know what you're doing here."

"All in good time, M'sieur Garson. For now, though, know this…if you'll give up this incompetent old fraud as your leader and let me take charge of you and your brothers and sisters, I promise that you'll not only go free and stay free, but you'll also have a chance to join a righteous cause…the liberation of the outer solar system, from here to Mars."

Garson frowned. "I'm not particularly interested in joining Starry Messenger, if that's what you're getting at."

"Then let me offer something else instead. You were brought down by Captain Future, weren't you?"

Garson's face reddened. "I don't like to talk about that," he muttered, looking away.

"I'm sure you don't." The Black Pirate's tone was sympathetic. "I imagine a number of people here don't like talking about him and the Futuremen. But I'm just as sure that all of you have a score to settle with them and wouldn't turn down a chance to get even…would you?"

Garson didn't answer. He didn't need to. His face said it all, just as it did for Athor Az and the other inmates. "If you'll join us," the Black Pirate went on, still speaking to Garson but addressing the others as well, "then you'll see Captain Future and the Futuremen dead. You might even get to pull the trigger yourself. Interested?"

"Hell, yeah, I'm interested," Garson replied. The others nodded.

"All right, then –" the Black Pirate jerked a thumb toward Corvo "–first, lock him up and don't let him out until I say so. Next, I need someone to show me –"

"Who are you?" Corvo demanded. Despite the gun at his head, he wanted to know who'd usurped his authority among his fellow prisoners.

The Black Pirate slowly turned about. For a moment or two, he calmly studied the former senator. Corvo had the distinct feeling that the man studying him was someone he knew, someone from his past. Someone like …

"Oh, my god." Corvo's next words were little more than a whisper. "It's you, isn't it?"

The Black Pirate's right hand rose to his mask. In one swift move, he yanked it from his head. Revealed was the face of a man believed to be dead…not only by Corvo, but also by Captain Future.

"Hello, Father," said Ul Quorn, the Magician of Mars. "Miss me?"

XI

A little more than an hour after Curt and the Futuremen concluded their council of war with Joan and Ezra, the *Comet* rose from its hangar. The little vessel became invisible as it rose above the crater wall and it remained that way until it reached orbital altitude, when Otho shut down the fantome and the ship became visible again. By then, the Brain had interfaced with the onboard navigation platform and put the ship on a rendezvous course with the warp torus in high orbit above the Moon.

Once the *Comet* was on final approach with the torus, Curt transmitted the code signal shutting down the warp module's fantome. Through the cockpit windows, the torus began to be visible as a small silver ring dangling in the moonlight. Curt took manual control of the *Comet* and gently guided it in, closing the distance meter by meter. As the sleek little vessel glided into the torus, its wingtips folded up into the vertical docking position. Simultaneously, the torus' anchor struts telescoped into position against the hull. A soft thump as the clamps automatically engaged, and the *Comet* was whole again.

It took just a few minutes for Curt, Otho and Simon to run through the warp drive checklist. Once it was finished, the Brain loaded his final calculations for the flight plan into the nav computer. Otho then initiated the five-minute launch countdown, and Curt began warming up the fusion main engine and the warp module, and slaved both to the *Comet's* AI system.

At T-minus ninety seconds, everything was handed over to the comps. Although Curt, Otho and the Brain continued to monitor the countdown, the *Comet's* AI net was in control. The task was too swift and complex for human, android, or even cyborg reflexes; only quantum AIs were capable of correctly making the split-second five-dimensional computations and actions necessary for the formation of an Alcubierre bubble. Curt accessed his Anni and used it to tell Joan, Ezra and Ashi, seated below in the passenger compartment, to check their seat harnesses, then he cinched his own straps a bit tighter and waited.

At T-minus sixty seconds, the *Comet's* main engine fired, breaking the ship out of lunar orbit and sending it outbound on a course slightly above the solar plane of the ecliptic. The *Comet* was unable to accelerate directly from parking orbit to subliminal velocity, hence the necessity of a fusion-drive boost. As the *Comet* began to accelerate, a subtle change occurred. Along the interior circumference of the torus, a slightly smaller inner ring parted from the outer ring. Tilting a few degrees out of alignment with each other, a superconductive electrical charge sent through the two rings began inducing the Casimir effect which would harness the dark energy that bonded the universe, quantum forces the *Comet* was able to tap into like water drawn from a cosmic well.

As the energy field grew, the warp bubble formed.

In theory, an Alcubierre drive could propel a spacecraft up to 100 times the speed of light. No one yet knew how to safely harness and control that much dark energy, though, so the *Comet's* warp torus was designed to generate only enough energy sufficient for .99c, just short of light speed. At T-minus-zero, the *Comet* went into warp. The main engine shut down, and for a stationary outside observer, it would have looked as if the little vessel suddenly leaped forward and disappeared in the blink of an eye. Earth fell away quickly, a tiny blue orb swiftly lost in an immense cosmos.

Even at .99c, though, it would take a little more than ten hours for the *Comet* to reach Pluto. Time enough for the truth to be told, for secrets to be revealed.

XII

" **A** ll right, lady," Ezra growled, "start talkin'…who's the Black Pirate?"

Once the *Comet* was enveloped by its warp bubble, artificial gravity was restored to the ship, a welcome side-effect of warp drive. Leaving Grag on the flight deck to stand watch, Curt, Otho and the Brain went below to join their passengers. Everyone was now gathered around the mess table, with coffee, tea, and English shortbread for those who consumed food and drink (Simon being the notable exception).

Ashi was seated at the center of the table, where all eyes were on her. She didn't answer at once, but instead quietly stroked the black and white tabby cat curled up in her lap. "She's really cute," she said to no one in particular. The cat contentedly purred. "What's her name?"

"Oog," Sitting beside her, Otho sipped at the mug of Darjeeling in his hand. "And that's not a cat."

"Of course it's a cat." Ashi gave him an annoyed look. "She's too old to be a kitten, if that's what you –"

"Think of another animal." Otho pointed to the small brown and white moondog sprawled across the deck below the table. "Eek, for instance. Picture him in your lap instead."

"I don't know why you…**what the hell?**"

As she spoke, the creature began to change. Without gaining or losing body size or mass, its muzzle elongated, its eyes grew smaller and closer together, its legs, paws, and tail became larger, and its fur became shorter and started to change color. Ashi yanked her hands away, and she stared in dumbstruck surprise as the cat rapidly transformed itself into another small dog, identical to the one on the floor.

Face pale with horror, Ashi leaped to her feet. The creature she'd assumed to be a cat fell from her lap. The moment it hit the floor, the transformation ceased and the creature suddenly became something else entirely: a soft, rubbery, off-white thing – eyeless, limbless, with orifices at each end – resembling an enormous insect larva. "Ooooog," it cooed as it developed a double-row of pseudopods along its underside and began to crawl away, unhurt by the fall.

"What…what …what …?" Ashi looked across the table at Curt.

"It's an anamorph." Curt was grinning at her bewilderment. "A shapechanger from Deneb, or at least that's where we assume it came from. We got him on Mars a few years ago…a little gift from your boss, Ul Quorn."

"And you didn't have to treat him so rough." Otho glared at her as he bent over to pick up Oog. The little Denebian again made the distinctive sound from which his – or rather, its – name was derived and settled into the android's lap instead. "It's okay, buddy," the android murmured, gently stroking it. "Some people just aren't nice to animals, that's all." He threw Ashi a hard look; she'd just given him another reason to dislike her.

Oog was Otho's pet, just as Eek was Grag's. Both had been found and adopted at about the same time five years ago, when Curt was pursuing the vendetta against Victor Corvo that had brought him and his compatriots into contact with Ul Quorn and Starry Messenger for the first time. Although they were often left behind when the *Comet* went on short missions, Oog and Eek were usually brought along when Curt and the others anticipated being away for a long time. Tycho Base had 'bots to take care of them, but Eek would get depressed and not touch his food if Grag was absent for a while.

As for Oog, its shapeshifting ability had been useful on more than one occasion, even if no one knew its purpose. Oog's very existence was a mystery. It was an artificial life form just as much as Otho was, but it obviously wasn't an android like him. And since it appeared to have been left behind by the Denebian explorers who'd visited the Moon and Mars in ancient times, that meant it was very likely over a million years old, making it virtually immortal. Was it a pet, then, or something else? Even Simon, who'd studied Oog as extensively as he could without killing and dissecting it – and he wouldn't even know how to go about doing that; nothing seemed to harm the creature, and it was capable of near-instantaneous cellular regeneration – could do little more than hypothesize about its reason for being.

"Enough about that critter." Irked by the distraction, Ezra Gurney glared at Ashi. "I asked you a question, and you ain't getting' off the hook that easy. So I'll ask you again…who's the Black Pirate?"

Ashi sighed. "He's…he's Ul Quorn," she said as she sat down again. Her voice was soft, her answer reticent.

"I knew it," Otho murmured.

Curt slowly nodded. Her answer should have been a surprise to them, but it really wasn't. Although it had widely been assumed that Ul Quorn was killed at the climax of that first encounter with Captain Future and the Futuremen, the fact remained that his body had never been found among those of the Sons of the Two Moons, the offshoot cult of Starry Messenger that was wiped out on Mars at its secret base in the caldera of the extinct Mons Ascraeus volcano.

Ashi noticed the muted reaction. "I take it this is something you expected?"

"Sort of." Joan picked up her tea, took a sip. "After the *Titan King* was hijacked, everyone the pirates put aboard lifeboats and jettisoned was interviewed by my people in IPF Section Four. One of them was the executive officer, the first person to meet the pirates when their ship was taken aboard the *King* under the pretense of a fake emergency."

Curt picked up the thread. "The XO said that, just before the Black Pirate made his appearance, a lady came off the ship the liner recovered. An aresian female whose description matched N'Rala, Ul Quorn's right-hand woman. And like Ul Quorn, her body was never found either."

As he spoke, Curt let his gaze drift to the porthole. At near-light speed, the stars had disappeared in front of the *Comet,* but were stretched out as multicolored rays alongside the ship, forming a luminous tunnel through which his vessel plunged. A beautiful and mesmerizing optical effect; he never got tired of it.

"We suspect," he went on, "that both Ul Quorn and N'Rala escaped aboard an air raft N'Rala flew into the vent of the volcano Starry Messenger was using as a base of operations. The last I saw of him, Ul Quorn was throwing himself into the volcano. Ascraeus Mons may be extinct, but the vent at the center of its caldera is a bottomless pit. If you jumped into it, you'd practically fall all the way to the core of the planet –"

"Unless you had an accomplice waiting to catch you with an air raft." Simon hovered at the end of the table, his eyestalks in constant motion as his carapace gently bobbed on its impellers. "So we've suspected for a while now that Ul Quorn and N'Rala didn't die at Ascraeus Mons, that the Magician of Mars pulled off one last trick –" a razzing sound from the speaker grill; the Brain's approximation of a laugh "– if you'll pardon the expression."

"Anyway," Curt said, "they managed that getaway just before my ship...my first ship, the *Comet I*...came down from orbit on autopilot and crashed in the volcano, blowing up the base and killing everyone there."

"No one has seen Ul Quorn or N'Rala since then," Otho said."But we've never bought the idea that they died." Folding his arms together, he shook his head in disgust. "So the bastard really is alive. Okay, I can accept that, but it doesn't tell us what he wants."

Joan shrugged. "One hundred million dollars is a lot of money."

"No," Ashi said, "he's right...that's not what Ul Quorn wants. Ransoming the *Titan King's* captain and the prison inmates is just a way to lure you to Pluto. "What he's really after –" she pointed across the table at Curt, "– is **you**."

"Me?" Curt was startled. "Are you saying that he's gone to all this trouble just because he wants revenge?"

Ashi nodded. "Yes, that's exactly what I mean. In fact, that's the reason I'm here."

"I don't follow. Why –?"

"When I joined Starry Messenger a couple of years ago, it wasn't long before they learned that you and I had once...had a relationship." Ashi blushed as she said this; from her end of the table, Joan glared at her. "When that came out, I was transported to Ceres, where Ul Quorn, N'Rala, and what was left of Starry Messenger's Martian cell fled after escaping you on Mars. When I told him how you and I knew each other when we were kids, he made me one of his lieutenants and put me in charge of the Starry Messenger cell on Stratos Venera. That's when we came up with the idea of sabotaging the rotarvator."

Ezra leaned forward across the table. "So the plot to blow up the rotarvator...that was just to get his attention?" A disgusted snort. "Killin' a whole lotta innocent folks is a helluva way to get in touch with an old boyfriend, kiddo."

"You'll eventually get a report about this from your people," Ashi said, "so you might as well hear it from me first. That charge we planted? A dud. Just enough dynatomite to register on radiation sensors, but it would've caused very little damage if it had blown up…which it wouldn't have, because the detonator was a dummy, too." She sighed. "I'm just sorry that one of the guys with me was killed. I was hoping it wouldn't come to that."

Curt remembered the Starry Messenger terrorist who'd fallen off the rotarvator platform after he'd stunned him with his plasma gun. It wasn't the first time Captain Future had taken a life in the line of duty, but he'd never killed someone so pointlessly. "So all that was just to get me to find you and take you into custody?"

Ashi nodded. "Ul Quorn is positively obsessed with you, Curt. Ever since you destroyed Starry Messenger's plans to lead a separatist revolution on Mars, he's wanted to get back at you. And this is it…having me help him lure you all the way out to the edge of the system, where you won't have the IPF and the Solar Coalition Navy to back you up."

"That's …" Curt began, but was interrupted by Ezra's voice coming to him through his Anni implant.

—Curt, Joan and I need to parlay with you in private.

—Can it wait? Curt asked.

This time, it was Joan who silently spoke to him. *—No, it can't. And I don't want that witch hearing what we have to tell you.*

—It concerns classified information, Ezra added. *—Now, son. And bring the others with you.*

Curt looked at Otho and the Brain. "I think we need to cut this short so we can rest a bit before we reach Pluto. Simon, Otho…would you join me on the flight deck, please?"

"And where would you like me to go?" Ashi asked.

Curt cocked his head toward Cabin Four, which he'd assigned to her. "I think you'll find your cabin a bit more comfortable than a prison cell…for the time being, at least."

XIII

"**C**urt, have you ever heard of the Slingshot Project?"

Ezra Gurney was sitting in the passenger seat directly behind Curt, who was in the pilot's chair. Joan was behind Otho, who was in the co-pilot's chair, while Simon had parked himself in his alcove in the cockpit's aft bulkhead. Four was the maximum number of people who could squeeze themselves onto the *Comet's* flight deck, not counting the Brain. Once more, Grag had been sent below to watch Ashi, who'd been locked in her cabin.

"Can't say that I have." Curt glanced at Joan. She shook her head, quietly letting him know that she hadn't either, or at least not until lately.

"Good, glad to hear it," Ezra said. "Means the security blackout IPF and the Science Ministry clamped down on the project has worked. We'll just have to hope that Ul Quorn hasn't heard about it either."

"But I suppose you're just dying to tell us," Otho said.

Ezra shook his head. "No, I'm not. And if things were different, I wouldn't have ever heard about it either. Fact is, Joan and I didn't know anything until Halk Anders called me on scrambler right after the breakout and briefed me. I let Joan in on things on the way to Tycho."

Once again, Curt noticed that, when Ezra Gurney spoke in earnest about serious matters, his looney accent disappeared, if only for a few minutes. He glanced at the pilot's control panel. The middle screen displayed the *Comet's* current position. The little ship was about to cross Saturn's orbit. In fact, if they'd been able to see anything through the bow windows except the starless black void straight ahead, Saturn and its largest moons would have been visible.

It occurred to Curt that Saturn and Pluto were presently in conjunction. Indeed, according to the screen's display of the respective orbits of the outer planets, Saturn and Pluto had been about five astronautical units closer to one another than their usual thirty AU median distance during the thirteen weeks that elapsed between the time the *Titan King* disappeared at Saturn and the time it reappeared near Pluto. Curt hadn't noticed this three months ago when he and the Futuremen had searched Saturn's moons and orbit for the hijacked liner...but then, it had never occurred to them to extend their search all the way out to the Kuiper Belt.

Was it a coincidence that the *Titan King* hijacking was tied to the Cold Hell breakout? Apparently not. Curt suspected that the two events were connected and things were about to get even stranger...and he was right.

"You remember the Dancing Denebians, don't you?" Ezra asked.

The marshal's question snapped Curt's attention back to the present. "Sure. The petroglyphs on the Moon, carved into the Straight Wall by explorers from Deneb about a million or so years ago."

"And also on Mars," Simon added. "In the caldera of Ascraeus Mons. Those are the ones Ul Quorn discovered. They helped him interpret the petroglyphs on the Moon."

"Right on both counts," Ezra said. "We were fortunate in that the Martian petroglyphs weren't destroyed along with just about everything else when you brought the *Comet* down on their heads." A slight smile. "It helped that they were carved into solid stone. The blast just 'bout obliterated everything else, but it 'pears that Martian rock is purty damn tough."

The looney accent was back. Ezra self-consciously laughed at his own joke and went on. "Well, once Ul Quorn told you how he'd interpreted the alien hieroglyphics and what all those lil' dancing stick-men stood for, and Simon here passed that info to the Science Ministry, their big brains went to work on translating them again. And this time, they were successful, now that they knew what to look for. Turns out that Ul Quorn was right about that, too. The Dancing Denebians on Mars were a mathematical expression for just about the biggest goddamn scientific secret humans have ever unlocked."

Joan picked up the thread. "The Martian petroglyphs explain how to create a tunnel through spacetime…a wormhole…that can instantly transfer a spacecraft from here to Deneb, just over 1,500 light-years from here."

Curt let out a long, low whistle, while a burst of static erupted from the Brain's speaker. On the other hand, Otho was skeptical. "A wormhole like that…look, I'm no physicist, but wouldn't that be difficult? I mean, the energy requirement alone –"

"Absolutely right, lad." At rest within his alcove, Simon's eyestalks flitted from one person to another. "Although naturally-occurring wormholes are somewhat common in interstellar space – they're thought to be a possible explanation for why a number of exoplanet probes have vanished over the years – creating an artificial wormhole has always been a daunting task for that reason. But since we've learned how to harness dark energy for warp drives, so doing the same thing to create a stable wormhole just entails a higher degree of difficulty, really."

"Yeah, sure…" Otho was skeptical.

"No, that's pretty much what Anders said when he briefed me," Ezra said. "And because Slingshot is considered to be just a leetle bit dangerous…not to mention Top Secret…it was decided to locate it as far as possible from anywhere else while still keeping it in the solar system."

"So they put it on Pluto," Curt said.

"Yup, you guessed it…right on Pluto. In fact, the spot they picked is Zheng He Montes, a mountain at the edge of the Sputnik Planum close to Cold Hell."

"Close enough, in fact," Joan said, "that a crawler could get there from the prison in just an hour or so. They placed it there so that the kuiperian settlement, Bernard's Landing, could provide material support for the lab."

Curt raised an eyebrow. "Including food?"

A wan smile. "No, the food supply comes from Cold Hell. The scientists eat the same thing the prisoners do, whatever is grown in the prison greenhouses. The kuiperian...um, diet...is restricted to what the natives eat themselves." Realizing that she'd just uttered an unintentional pun, Joan turned red. "So to speak," she added.

Curt let it pass. "Do the inmates know about Slingshot?"

"Nope," Ezra replied. "All they know is that some of the vegetarian food they produce in Cold Hell goes to Bernard's Landing for the kuiperians, who in turn provide support for the prison. Almost no one at the prison knew anything about Slingshot, and since they were senior staff like Warden Jeerdin, we can safely assume that they're dead."

"And if we're lucky," Joan went on, "it'll stay that way and Ul Quorn won't find out about it." Her expression darkened. "But we can't take that chance. If he and Starry Messenger knew about the Slingshot Project when they cooked up this mess –"

"You're beginning to sound like Ezra." Curt give her a wink that managed to produce a brief smile.

"But even if Ul Quorn **does** know about Slingshot," the Brain said, "it doesn't explain some of the actions he and his followers have taken. Why hijack the *Titan King*? Why take and hold hostages? Why disguise himself? Why –?"

"Why get that woman involved?" Although Joan didn't utter Ashi Lanyr's name, everyone knew whom she was talking about. "Sure, I know what she just told us, but there's still something about her story that doesn't add up." She looked at Curt. "I know the two of you had an adolescent fling," she went on, and Curt felt his face become warm, "but don't trust her, Curt. Don't trust her, and don't you dare turn your back on her."

"I know. Believe me, I learned that a long time ago." Curt looked from Joan to Otho and Simon. "No matter what happens, we're not letting her off this ship, and we can't let Ul Quorn or any of her people know that she's with us. Understood?"

"Absolutely, son," the Brain said. Otho nodded in agreement.

"All right, then." Curt glanced again at the navigation screen. In just the short time they'd been speaking, the *Comet* had rushed past Uranus's orbit. Steadily rising above the solar plane of the ecliptic, the ship would soon be passing Neptune's orbit. In just a few hours, the *Comet* would be entering the Kuiper Belt, with Pluto its final destination.

"Let's start making plans," he said. "I think I have an idea or two of what we ought to do…"

XIV

The *Comet* came out of warp 250,000 miles from Pluto, the minimum safe distance for deceleration from sub-light speed. Dawn was just breaking over the minor planet's western hemisphere where Cold Hell was located, but were it not for the icy reflectivity caused by the permanent glaciers that covered most of its surface, Pluto's daylight hours would have been dim as well as frigid. As it was, the little world looked like an old softball some adolescent god lost in the solar system's outfield and gave up trying to find.

This was the first time Curt had seen Pluto with his own eyes. Captain Future had caused many men and women to be sent here by a judge and jury, but until now, there had never been a reason for him to visit this cold and lonely little world. As the *Comet* finished its deceleration burn and made its 180-degree forward turn, the part of him who relished exploring new places wanted to set down in some region where neither *Homo sapiens* nor *Homo cosmos* had ever set foot before and…just walk around, see what was to be seen. But he couldn't. There was a job that needed to be done; like it or not, he was the man to do it.

Every now and then, Curt resented being Captain Future. This was one of those times…

"There's the *Titan King*," Otho said.

Curt came out of his reverie to look where the android was pointing. At first he didn't see anything, but when he peered more closely, he made out a bright, tiny star moving just above the eastern limb of the planetoid. It couldn't be anything else but an orbiting spacecraft, and a pretty large one at that.

"It's the *King*, all right." Curt bent forward to manipulate the trackball of the cockpit's virtual telescope. Using the center-left screen, he located the moving star with the viewfinder, then expanded the image to its maximum size. Otho leaned across his seat to watch as the *Titan King* leaped into view.

By and large, the space liner that the hijackers had rechristened the *Liberator* looked the same except for the bow.

"What **is** that thing?" Otho murmured, pointing to the intricate scaffold that had replaced the observation dome at the ship's bow. "Is it...I dunno, a telescope, maybe?"

"Maybe," Curt said even though he knew Otho's conjecture was nothing more than a wild guess. The bow structure didn't look like any sort of radiotelescope he'd ever seen, not even an x-ray observatory. It had clearly been built with some purpose in mind; it might even be the reason why the *Titan King* had been taken in the first place. But he was damned if he knew what that might be. Indeed, Curt doubted he'd be able to figure it out even if they got closer...and getting closer wasn't the part of the plan.

"Okay," he said to Otho, "your turn. Go below and get started." He checked the ship's chronometer. "We've got about an hour and half to go before we hit the deadline, and it'll take about half that time for approach and landing. Think you can do what you need to do by then?"

"Easy." Otho unfastened his harness, floated out of his seat. "The Brain said he'll give me a hand. That'll make things faster."

"Let me know when you're ready and we'll run a little test."

"Okey-doke. See you soon."

Weightless again, Otho pushed himself toward the manhole leading to the *Comet's* lower deck. Alone in the cockpit, Curt turned his attention to putting his ship in orbit around Pluto.

He refrained from engaging the fantome, at least for now. He wanted the *Liberator* to see that the *Comet* had arrived. Ul Quorn and his crew had probably spotted the little ship already; the prolonged flare of the *Comet's* fusion engines during the deceleration burn had created a bright, moving torch against the stars that would've been hard to miss. But Curt also wanted to be careful not to expose the warp torus to view, so as he swung the ship in closer to Pluto, he also selected a course that would put the *Comet* in geostationary orbit above the planetoid's equator but would keep it on the other side of Pluto from the *Liberator*.

As he worked, Curt heard someone quietly come up from below. He glanced over his shoulder; yes, it was Joan. He gave her a brief nod and smile, but she didn't respond in kind. Without a word, she slipped into the co-pilot's seat. She knew better than to distract him; instead, she quietly watched as he set the autopilot for where he wanted to go. She'd wanted to talk with him about something; Curt had little doubt what it was.

Without Otho's or Simon's assistance, it took a little more effort than usual to separate the *Comet* from its warp torus. But he managed to do so, and once the lander was free, Curt activated the torus's fantome generator. He watched as the torus faded from sight; when he reached over to activate the transponder that would help him locate it again, Joan surprised him a little by doing it for him.

"Where did you learn to do that?" he asked.

A soft smile. "Seriously? You don't think I've sat behind you all this time and not learned a trick or two?"

"Yeah, I guess I should've known. So, what's up? Why are you –?"

"Who is she, Curt? I guess you don't like me asking, but I think I have a right to know. What is she, an old girlfriend or something?"

"Old girlfriend. Knew her when we were kids." Curt was surprised to find how reluctant he was to discuss Ashi Lanyr with Joan, but she was right; he had an obligation to tell her about Ashi, and not only because of Lt. Joan Randall's official role as Captain Future's IPF liaison. "It's a long story," he began, "but here goes…"

Curt made it brief, but nonetheless, he explained things as thoroughly as he could, going back to when he and Ashi had first met, when they were teenagers and Curt was visiting Venus's Venera Stratos colony for the first time. He avoided confessing that he'd once been in love with Ashi or that he still had certain feelings for her, but the unsmiling expression on Joan's face, the penetrating look in her eyes, told him that she'd figured that out anyway. But she didn't say anything until he was done, and by then, it was almost time for the *Comet* to make its descent to Pluto's surface.

"I see," Joan said once he'd finished, "and I think I understand." With a small sigh, she turned her head to gaze out the porthole window. "I just want to know one thing…I'm not going to have to worry about your love for her –"

"I'm not in love with her, Joan. Not any more."

"– getting in the way of the mission, am I?" She turned to him again, her gaze both direct and unfathomable. "Am I?"

"No, I –"

"Good. That's all I need to know." Joan unfastened the waist strap and pushed herself up and out of the seat. "Okay, let's go below and see how that test of yours is working out."

"Hold on. Let me make sure with Otho that it's all right to come down." Curt reached out to the android through his Anni link. *–Otho, are you ready?*

–Sure, chief. Come on down. I'm in her cabin.

–Has she figured it out yet?

–Nope. I've been in here for the last five minutes, and she doesn't seem to notice.

–Okay. I'll be there in a sec.

Curt backed out of Anni, turned to Joan again. "So far, so good." He grinned. "Let's go mess with my old girlfriend's head."

A wry smile from Joan, but she didn't reply.

Together, they made their way down to the *Comet's* lower deck. Curt and Joan used handrails to move about in weightlessness, but once they reached the cabin they'd assigned Ashi, they planted their stikshoes against the floor. Grag stood outside Cabin Four; since he could magnetize the soles of his feet at will, he almost floated weightless and apparently didn't miss not sharing that particular human pleasure.

On the other hand, he did occasionally experience boredom. "Am I going to spend this whole mission doing nothing more than watching this woman?" Grag asked Curt as soon as he came down. "There are other things I could be doing, you know."

"Sorry, old friend. Didn't mean to stick you with this job for so long." Curt contemplated the cabin door for a moment. "Has she ever tried to open it without your permission?"

"No." Grag shook his head. "She knocks when she needs to visit the head or gets hungry or thirsty, but she's never tested the lock or misbehaved. And that door is solid, Curt. Even I would have some trouble breaking it down."

Curt nodded. As a 320-A series construction 'bot, Grag was built for tough jobs. Once during a mission that had taken the Futuremen to China, Curt saw him pick up a half-ton hovercraft and throw it at the lifewater smugglers who'd had him, Grag and Ezra pinned down in a firefight. And Cabin Four was designed with possible prisoners in mind; once locked from outside, it would take a retinal scan or a code number to open it. If Grag said Ashi couldn't force her way out, then the 'bot was to be believed.

"Okay, pal," he said. "So long as she's locked up tight while we're not around, then you don't have to stay out here the whole time. And I'll probably need you once we land."

"Thanks, Curt." Grag stepped out of the way. "You can go in now."

Joan chuckled. "Thank you, Captain Grag."

"Don't mention it, sweetheart."

It took another minute for Curt and Joan to stop laughing. Once they'd straightened themselves out, Curt took a deep breath, exhaled, and looked at Joan. "Ready?" he asked, and when she nodded, he grasped the door handle and slid it open.

Ashi was floating weightless above her bed, long legs tucked up against her chest, arms wrapped about her knees. She'd been having a conversation with the previous person who'd come to visit her, a good-looking man a little younger than herself whose red hair was tied back in a short ponytail and whose handsome face had the bronzed tan of someone who'd spent a lot of time wearing a space helmet. Her eyes turned to Curt as he entered the cabin. Then she glanced at her first visitor. Then she stared at Curt again, and this time her eyes widened and her mouth fell open.

"Hello, Curt," said Curt.

Otho turned to look at him. "Hello, Curt," he replied, giving him an easy smile.

Stunned, Ashi's gaze moved again from one person to the next. "What...who ...?"

"Is something wrong?" Otho asked, looking at her again. Curt was pleased to hear his own voice come from the android's mouth. "Don't you recognize your old boyfriend?"

Curt regarded Otho with mock astonishment. "Now don't confuse the poor lady, Curt. You know who I am! I'm Otho!"

"Oh, no you don't," Otho exclaimed. "I'm Otho, and you're Curt!"

"Uh-uh, no way. **I'm** Otho, and **you're** ..."

"Shut up! Both of you!" Although Joan was laughing. Ashi was far from amused. She glared at the two men, human and android, standing before her. "This isn't funny," she said angrily. "I think it's a mean trick."

"Maybe," Curt said, "but you've got to admit, it's pretty good." He stepped closer to Otho until they were side by side, their shoulders almost touching. "Okay, let's see if you can figure out which is which."

Ashi unfolded herself from the compact ball she'd made of herself. She studied both of them for a few moments, carefully looking them up and down. Curt knew that it wouldn't be easy to tell him and Otho apart. Over the years, the android had perfected this little trick. It wasn't just a red wig, skin-toning lotion – two shades: a darker one for his face, a slightly lighter one for hands, neck, and forearms – and gray contact lenses for his eyes. The one-piece jumpsuit he wore was subtly padded to add the illusion of more muscle, and the soles of his boots were elevated to subtly increase his height. Otho had even studied Curt's mannerisms, the physical and verbal quirks that, under normal circumstances, made him unique. And if anything, Curt's voice was the easiest thing to duplicate…for an android, at least.

There was just one crucial difference, one small problem that couldn't be easily solved. The only person to discover it so far had been Joan. She figured out how to tell Curt and Otho apart by giving each of them a kiss; Curt knew how to kiss a woman, but Otho didn't. It might occur to Ashi to make the same test, but with Joan in the room, it would be dangerous for her to even try.

Instead, Ashi lowered her feet so that her stikshoes adhered to the floor, then walked over to where Otho stood and raised her hand, offering a handshake. With a knowing smile, Otho shook her hand.

"Hello, Otho," she said to the android, then she looked at Curt. "Nice try, but he needs to always wear gloves when he does that. His hand is cold as ice."

"Well, I wouldn't say it's **that** cold," Otho said, speaking now in his normal voice, "but, yes, subnormal epidermal temperature is something we've never been able to get around."

"Still, it's a good trick, I'll give you that." Ashi looked at Curt again. "Use it often?"

"Sometimes." He didn't want to tell her that he and Otho had devised this little gag a few years ago when it was necessary for Captain Future to be in two places at once. They'd done it several times since then, and each time Otho had gotten a little better at pulling off the impersonation.

Curt glanced at his wristband. Their deadline was just twenty minutes away. "Okay, guys, fun's over. Otho, you, Joan, and Simon go up top. Grag, Ezra, come with me."

"And where are you going?" Ashi said, almost as much a demand as a question.

Curt ignored her as he kicked off from the floor, grabbed hold of the ceiling rail, and headed for the adjacent ready-room. The less she knew, the better...

XV

During the *Comet's* next orbit, while the little ship was on the other side of Pluto from both the *Liberator* and Cold Hell, the recon pod was deployed. The spherical little craft quickly descended toward the frozen world below, forming a thin plasma shell around itself as it plummeted through the thin atmosphere. If the pod had been deployed within sight of the pirate vessel or the prison, someone would have doubtless spotted the pod as it made atmospheric entry; not even its fantome generator could have prevented that. And it was important that Ul Quorn and his people remain unaware that Captain Future – the **real** Captain Future – was not aboard the *Comet*, but somewhere else instead.

With Ezra "riding shotgun" – another pet expression of the marshal's that he thought no one understood but himself; Curt did, but only because he watched a lot of twentieth century movies – Curt piloted the pod as it made its steep descent, not leveling off until they were just 1,500 feet above the ground. By then, they were above the southwestern corner of Viking Terra due west of the Zheng He mountains, at the foot of which Bernard's Landing and the Slingshot Project were located.

–I suggest that we land at Bernard's Landing, Ezra said via Anni. *–The kuiperians I know there will take us to the lab and make introductions.*

Like Curt, he wore a bulky EE suit, so densely insulated against the cold that it resembled one of the NASA Apollo spacesuits that the first lunar explorers wore. Their helmets, transparent lunaglass bubbles protected by hoods, didn't have faceplates that could be raised or lowered, making it necessary for them to communicate with each other either by radio or neural net.

–And you don't think we ought to go straight to the lab? As Curt spoke, he steered the pod with the lever-like hand controllers mounted on either side of his seat.

–We could, but it be just a leetle bit risky. I wouldn't bet against Ul Quorn already knowing about Slingshot. And if he does,

then he and his gang may've found that lab already. You don't wanna take a chance of them pouncin' on us soon as we land, do you?

–*No.* Curt thought about it a moment. –*But if that's the case, wouldn't his gang land first at Bernard's Landing?*

–*And introduce themselves to the locals, hopin' they'll be friends?* Ezra laughed. –*Son, nobody makes friends with kuiperians!*

–*You did.*

–*That's 'cause I'm such a nice, easy-going fella.* Ezra winked at him through his helmet. –*And I didn't believe all the stories people say 'bout them. They appreciated that.*

Curt knew what he meant. Everyone in the system knew the legend of Bernard's Landing.

Many years ago, when the newly-formed Solar Coalition decided to make Pluto the site of its maximum security prison, it sent an expedition to the Kuiper Belt, the first ever to set foot on the cold little world at the edge of the solar system. Led by famed British space explorer Graham Bernard, the expedition landed at the western side of the Tombaugh Regio near the Sputnik Planum. A hundred and fifty men and women were in the expedition, which made the long journey from Earth aboard the *SCS Damon Knight*, an immense fusion-powered colony ship that spent nearly a year in space before finally reaching its destination.

The expedition had been on Pluto for a little more than ten weeks, and had begun work on transforming a giant iceberg into what would become known as Cold Hell, when disaster struck. The *Knight,* still in orbit above Pluto, suffered a major incident when the primary coolant system of its main reactor suddenly failed. Within minutes, the handful of crewmen still aboard the ship – none of whom were engineers who could've handled the emergency – lost control of the reactor. They barely had time to alert the colony when it exploded, transforming the *Knight* into a miniature supernova that briefly outshone the distant Sun.

All at once, Bernard's Landing no longer had its primary means of support. The colony hadn't yet become self-sufficient and still depended on the *Knight* for many things…in particular, most of the colonists' food, since it was stored in temperature-controlled freezers where it could be defrosted and shuttled down to the surface whenever the pantries needed to be restocked. A greenhouse was being built, but it wasn't yet finished; the first crops hadn't been planted, so there weren't any fresh vegetables that could be harvested. And an inventory gave the colonists further bad news: even with strict emergency rationing, they had less than one month's supply for a hundred and fifty people before the food ran out. To make matters worse, the rescue ship, the *SCS Kate Wilhelm*, was still three weeks away from being launched from Earth orbit, and wouldn't get to Pluto for another eleven months.

Through the ages, cannibalism has been a way many marooned and shipwrecked people have managed to stay alive. The *Essex* whaling ship disaster of 1820, the Donner Party horror of 1864, and the 1972 crash of Uruguayan Air Force Flight 571 are but a few notable examples. When humankind began to colonize space, it was only a matter of time before it happened there, too. What occurred on Pluto was preceded by tragic incidents on Mars and Ganymede in the late 21st and early 22nd centuries, before the Alcubierre warp drive made fast interplanetary rescue missions possible.

But warp drives hadn't yet been perfected when the *Knight* expedition went to Pluto; they'd have to wait until the *Wilhelm* arrived. The colonists – baseline *Homo sapiens* preceding the advent of *Homo cosmos* – soon came to grips with the fact that they'd run out of sufficient food to feed all of their number long before the rescue ship would reach them, and even with a finished greenhouse, they'd soon be starving; their crops could only grow so fast. It wasn't enough to simply reduce their population enough to live off the dwindling supply of rations they still had. The sacrifice had to go further than that…much further, into dark territories that few people like to even think about, let alone step into. And yet, it was clear that, if the majority were to survive, a few would have to die and pass along their bodies for the consumption of those they left behind.

It was Graham Bernard himself who took the first step. Late one evening, after everyone else had gone to sleep, the expedition leader sat alone in his quarters and wrote a letter, explaining his actions and giving explicit instructions about what had to be done once he was gone. Then he went to the nearest airlock, put on an EE suit but left off the helmet, then stepped into the chamber and gradually decompressed it without triggering the fail-safes or opening the outer hatch. Death came quickly and with relatively little pain; the first breath of Pluto's carbon dioxide atmosphere killed him within seconds. The suit prevented his body from freezing solid, though, which was what Bernard wanted: to leave behind a fresh corpse that could be harvested by the people he'd once led.

The inhabitants of Bernard's Landing – as the new colony was renamed in his memory – weren't savages. After a memorial service was held, a small group of volunteers that included one of the colony's doctors carefully dissected Bernard's body, cutting it apart and preserving the pieces known to be edible. They'd done their research and thus knew that the brain shouldn't be consumed lest it produce kuru disease; likewise, the gall bladder was discarded as poisonous. The rest, though, was cooked just as if it were the central ingredient of a meat stew, seasoned with spices and mixed with canned vegetables from the colony's dwindling stock. Today, the recipe is commonly known as Graham stew, a traditional meal served on the kuiperian holiday known as Survivors Day.

Many of the colonists refused to share that first meal. Some preferred to commit suicide themselves rather than descend to such depravity. When they did, their bodies were harvested, too. There's no truth to the part of the legend that says the colonists murdered one another for food. Every colonist who was later consumed took his or her own life, with several following Bernard's example, sacrificing themselves so that others might live.

By the time the *Wilhelm* finally arrived, twenty-three colonists had perished, either by their own hands or from natural causes, and become food for those who still lived; at that point, there wasn't one among them who hadn't tasted human flesh, however reluctantly. It was the reactions of the crew of the *Wilhelm* that made them realize that they could never return to Earth, not without being reviled and persecuted for violating one of the oldest and strongest of human taboos. So the survivors of the *Knight* remained on Pluto, and cannibalism became part of kuiperian culture.

Like other offshoots of humankind,, the first native-born generation of *Homo cosmos kuiperian* were genetically modified to suit their environment. For them, it was having the pancreas modified to produce enzymes better capable of digesting the flesh of their own kind. Their teeth were altered to provide larger and sharper cuspids suited for a carnivorous diet, giving them small fangs that were occasionally visible depending on facial expression. Their skin was protected by fine, pelt-like hair, including their faces; they often dyed their facial hair into patterns, both simple and elaborate, meant to identify themselves and their beliefs, interests or occupations. Both men and women had facial hair; bearded women were not uncommon in kuiperian culture.

"They look wild, but they're actually pretty nice once you get to know 'em," Ezra commented as he and Curt flew low across the frozen wilderness. "So long as you treat 'em with common courtesy and respect, you'll never have to worry about 'em sneakin' up on you with a steak knife."

Curt shivered inside his suit, a sudden chill that didn't come from the frigid cockpit. "I'll try to keep that in mind. So what's the name of your friend again?"

"Elizabeth Nourse, though she goes by another name. Livereatin' Lil, she's called."

"Sounds charming."

"She is, really. Kuiperians adopt nicknames like that. Old custom. Anyway, she's the law here. I met her when she came to Luna for IPF basic training way back when. She's now in charge of the local IPF garrison."

"And she'll escort us to the research lab?"

"She should. Providin' security for Slingshot is part of her job. Without her, we're not gonna so much as set foot in the door." Ezra gave him a sidelong look through his helmet. "And if Ul Quorn knows about Slingshot —"

"There's a chance he's already made it to the lab," Curt finished. "In which case, we're going to need all the help we can get."

"Yup." Ezra nodded. "But Lil knows her stuff. Hell, she was one of the best rookies I've ever trained. So if Starry Messenger has taken the lab, she'll be our best chance of shakin' 'em loose."

Curt didn't respond, instead focusing his attention on the controls. They'd just passed over a range of icy hills; straight ahead, as far as the eye could see, were the rilles and crater-pocked badlands that lay east of the Zheng He Montes. Less than a hundred or so miles to go; already the mountains were in sight. Pushing the control bar forward, he descended to 500 feet, hugging the terrain in order to pass beneath the local radar that would pick up the pod.

He and Ezra would be arriving at Bernard's Landing in just fifteen or twenty minutes. Curt hoped the old marshal was right about where his former student's loyalties lay. And if that wasn't enough to worry about, he caught himself fretting over how the rest of his team would fare once they reached the prison.

The *Comet* would be touching down at Cold Hell any minute now...

XVI

From outward appearances, nothing about the prison seemed amiss. Lights gleamed within the tesseracts, turrets and hollowed-out glacial bluffs comprising the sections of Cold Hell that were visible aboveground. Otho flew the *Comet* in a low, tight circle about the prison, but neither he nor Joan spotted anything unusual. The violence that occurred here was entirely within its icy walls. No one had brought the bodies outside to be left for the locals; the crucified skeletons had no new companions.

"There's our touchdown point." Seated in the co-pilot's chair, Joan pointed to the landing field that lay just outside the prison. Aside from the delta-winged passenger shuttle from the *Titan King* incongruously parked beside the dome-like hangars holding the prison's own spacecraft, there were no other vessels on the field. But Ul Quorn had instructed them to look out for a mark that would be painted where the *Comet* was to touch down, and sure enough, there it was: the letters "CF" within a circle, painted red in the middle of the landing field not far from the hangars.

"I see it." Otho made another circle of the prison, studying the field before committing them. "I don't see anyone down there, do –?"

"Sputnik Planitia Penal Colony to approaching spacecraft." The voice that came through their headsets was electronically filtered as it had been before; Ul Quorn was still carrying on the pretense of being the Black Pirate. "Unidentified craft, this is Sputnik Planitia PC. Respond and identify yourself at once. Over."

"Okay," Joan said quietly, "you're on."

Otho touched his headset. When he spoke again, it was with Curt's voice. "Sputnik Planitia, this is *SCS Comet,* Captain Future speaking. Please identify yourself. Over."

Joan and Otho had decided not to let Ul Quorn know that they'd deduced whose face was behind the Black Pirate's mask. Whatever the reason the Magician of Mars had for hiding his identity, they'd continue to pretend ignorance for a little while longer, until the ransom was paid and the hostages were released. Both Otho and Ul Quorn were carrying on a masquerade; the question was, which of them would drop his mask first?

"This is the person you've chosen to call the Black Pirate," Ul Quorn replied. "It's an honor to speak with you, Captain Future...or shall we go by your real name?"

"He's testing you," Joan whispered. "Wants to see if you're really whom you say you are."

Otho nodded; he'd figured that out as well. "You can call me Curt if you wish. And what name should I use for you?"

A brief laugh, made harsh by electronic distortion. "Touché. Nice try, M'sieur Newton, but I think I prefer to remain anonymous for the time being." Then his tone became businesslike. "Here are your instructions. You will descend to the landing field, touching down on the mark with your port side airlock facing the prison. Before you land, you will open your weapons blisters, deploy your guns so that we can see them, and point them toward the sky. By the same token, you will keep your torpedo tubes closed. Any attempt to use your weapons and the hostages will die."

"Who are the other hostages?" Otho asked. "You told us you have Captain Lamont...who's the other one?"

"Senator Victor Corvo is now our prisoner as well." Again, a brief and humorless laugh. "You may not owe the senator any favors, but I doubt President Carthew will be pleased if you allow a former elected official to be killed...even a disgraced one like Corvo."

Otho and Joan traded an astonished look. The last inmate of Cold Hell they expected Ul Quorn to threaten was his own father. Before either of them could say anything, though, they heard Simon's voice behind them.

"Best go along with their demands," said the Brain, who'd floated up from below unnoticed. "I hate to say it, but we can't let them kill Corvo, too."

Unspoken but understood was the fact that Victor Corvo was responsible for the murders of Roger and Elaine Newton. Not only were they Curt's parents, but also Simon Wright's former students and friends. Even if the Brain was able to shed a tear, he had none for Corvo. Nonetheless, he knew that letting Corvo die by the hand of his illegitimate son would carry a cost; some might claim that James Carthew let Captain Future settle a vendetta against a former political foe. In any case, Ul Quorn had them in a box.

"Understood," Otho said. "Go on."

"Finally, once you've landed, you will exit your ship unarmed. You'll be permitted to wear EE gear, of course, but no guns or weapons will be in your hands or on your person. Also, you must bring with you every person aboard. This includes IPF Lt. Joan Randall, who is known to frequently travel with you. No person will be allowed to remain aboard the *Comet* until the ransom has been paid and the hostages have been freed. Do you understand?"

"Damn it," the Brain said quietly.

That was Joan's sentiment as well. Since Otho was playing at being Curt, there was no way he could physically be present as two people at the same time.

"Why do you want us to do that?" Otho asked, still mimicking Curt's voice. "Don't you trust us?"

"Frankly, no," replied Ul Quorn, and this time he didn't laugh. "If I can see everyone who's aboard, then I'll know for certain that you won't cross us."

"I understand," Otho replied, "but we need to have assurance that you won't cross us either. After all, you're the one holding hostages, not us." He paused a moment, letting this sink in. "Allow Otho to remain aboard. And our robot, too. You have my solemn word they won't touch our weapons while we're here, or act in any way to interfere with the payment of ransom for hostages. Also, our robot needs to perform some engine maintenance while we're gone, and he… it…requires Otho's supervision. Agreed?"

Joan held her breath. Otho was playing a bluff that might or might not work. If Ul Quorn called his bluff, they wouldn't have any recourse but to admit the truth: Curt wasn't actually aboard the *Comet*, and it was really Otho himself who was pretending to be Captain Future.

They also needed to leave Grag behind, although not for the reason given, but to stand guard over Ashi Lanyr. She may have been securely locked in Cabin Four, but leaving her alone in the *Comet* was not a wise idea.

Seconds crawled by. The *Comet* continued to slowly circle the prison and its landing field. The landing field was still deserted. There didn't seem to be anyone down there. Still...

"Very well, then," Ul Quorn said, "your request is granted. The android and the 'bot can stay aboard while the others come out."

Joan let out a relieved sigh; she hastily stifled it behind her hand, lest it be heard over the comlink. "Thank you," Otho replied, keeping calm. "We'll be landing in five minutes. *Comet* over and out."

He switched off the com, giving Joan and Simon a quick look. "That was close."

"It still is." Simon's eyestalks swiveled toward him. "But we know one thing, at least. He didn't ask to see Ashi Lanyr, which means that he doesn't know she's aboard."

"Good. Let's keep it that way." Otho reached down to the center console and flipped a set of toggle switches. A loud whir and a thump could be heard from underneath the hull as the landing gear dropped into position. "Okay, keep your fingers crossed," he said. "We're going in."

XVII

Bernard's Landing resembled an immense bullseye four miles in diameter, a low white dome with clear horizontal sections interspersed by concentric black rings spreading outward from the center. The clear sections were skylights, the black circles were radiators installed to prevent a greenhouse effect within the habitat. Situated at the foot of the Zheng He Montes, the colony was elevated upon a thick stem a half-mile wide, with cathedral-like buttresses spaced about the circumference providing additional support. Surrounding the main dome were a collection of smaller domes connected by enclosed tramways.

It was said that Pluto was a world someone could visit without ever setting foot outside, and to a certain extent, this was true. Most native kuiperians avoided leaving Bernard's Landing except when necessary; even with genetic modifications and insulated EE suits, emerging from the dome was a dangerous undertaking. Hypothermia was the leading cause of death on Pluto, one that could sneak up without warning and kill even a wary native, and no one wanted to be prematurely consumed by their family and friends.

The spaceport was a short distance from the colony, a leveled field with only a few surface structures; hangars, warehouses, and port authority were mainly underground. Curt set the recon pod down on the landing pad designated by traffic control. He didn't identify himself, letting Ezra do the talking. Ezra identified himself as Doc Walker and Curt as Rab Cain, and claimed that they were a pair of merchantmen. When Ezra texted a priority request for a meeting with Security Chief Nourse, though, the port authority officer on duty recognized the code numbers and phrases the marshal inserted in the header identifying him as belonging to IPF Section Four; he replied that Livereating Lil would meet them at the spaceport.

The landing pad was an elevator platform above an underground hangar. As the platform slowly descended, the doors closed and the hangar repressurized. Once the platform came to a halt, a recorded voice told them that they were free to disembark, but recommended that they wear cold weather gear. Even pressurized and heated to a habitable temperature, the thermometer stood at 14 degrees F.

Curt and Ezra climbed out of the pod and waddled across the hangar to the airlock. Their EE hardsuits were thick and cumbersome, and it was only Pluto's light gravity that allowed them to move at all. Since the hangar was already pressurized, they needed only to pass through the airlock's outer and inner doors to reach the ready-room on the other side, where a pair of kuiperian techs waited to help them out of the one-piece suits.

A kuiperian woman and her aresian male companion were waiting for them outside the ready room. Livereating Lil stood just a little more than five feet tall, stocky as all kuiperians were. Her long hair, dark gray and coiled up into a thick bun at the back of her neck, blended well with her downy facial hair, which was dyed a light shade of blue and intricately patterned with whorls and curlicues. Curt couldn't see much else of her because of the IPF uniform she wore, but he had little doubt that her body décor extended to the rest of her.

"Ezra Gurney!" she exclaimed, blowing into her palms before clasping the old lawman's hand: the traditional kuiperian greeting, sharing body warmth. "How long has it been?"

"Too long, Lil. Too long." Ezra reciprocated her two-handed handshake, symbolically returning her warmth with his own. "You've gone far for a lady who once almost shot her foot off during basic training."

"Oh hush, you. I seem to remember you making a pass at a certain aresian lady." She favored him with a wink; her remark was an inside joke only the two of them understood.

"Never happened, never happened." Ezra grinned and shook his head, then turned to Curt. "Allow me to introduce an old friend. He's –"

"Captain Future. Of course I know who he is. Just because we live underground doesn't mean we live under a rock." Stepping over to Curt, Lil opened her hands to him. "It's an honor to meet you, sir. I've been an admirer for years."

"Thank you," Curt clasped Livereating Lil's hands with his own, and tried not to picture this gentle, hirsute woman feasting on human flesh.

"May I introduce my second-in-command?" Lil turned to the tall aresian standing quietly nearby. "This is Lt. Lom Vega. He comes to us through IPF's Officer Exchange Program and has been serving in my garrison for the past four months."

"A pleasure to meet you both." Lom had learned kuiperian customs during his time here, but not to the point of letting his black hair grow out or cultivating a beard. His head was entirely hairless save for his eyebrows, making him to resemble Otho with a deep tan. "Particularly you, Captain Future. Your reputation preceedes you."

"Thank you." Curt returned the double-handshake before turning to Livereating Lil again. "I wish we had time for pleasantries, but our business is urgent. You're aware of the prison uprising, of course, and the demands their leader has made."

"Of course." Lil's smile faded, although the sharp tips of her elongated cuspids remained visible. "But if you've come to Pluto to deliver the ransom, you're in the wrong place. You should've landed at the prison, not here."

"Actually, I **am** at Cold Hell…or rather, someone who looks like me is."

Lil stared at him. "How –?"

"Never mind that now." Curt waved off the question. "For the present, our main concern is the Slingshot Project."

"Certainly, but why do you think it's threatened? The prison inmates know nothing about it. Even if they did, I doubt they'd care."

"We think the uprising has been staged by Starry Messenger and that it's only a cover for their real objective…getting their hands on Slingshot." Curt gestured to the door. "If you'll lead us to whatever mode of transportation you normally use to reach the lab, I'll tell you the rest along the way."

"Please do, but I'd be remiss if I didn't offer you lunch first."

"Umm…"

A tiger-like smile, accompanied by a short laugh. "We're not totally cannibalistic," Livereating Lil said. "Actually, our diet is largely vegetarian. We grow most of our food, and when we do consume flesh, it's usually the remains of a friend or relative who has died by accident, old age, or from natural causes. We never kill someone just to eat them."

"Forgive me, but I've heard otherwise. Isn't Cold Hell surrounded by the skeletons of inmates who escaped and were captured?"

"That's true," Lom said, answering for Lil before she had the chance, "except that those escapees weren't captured by her people. They tried to make their way here on foot. But you'll freeze to death in an ordinary vacuum suit, which is all they can usually get their hands on."

"So when my people locate escaped prisoners," Lil said, "usually they're already dead. We turn the bodies over to the charnel house as food for the indigent members of our community. The only thing we ask that they return the skeleton to us and not make use of it as well – bones make excellent hand tools, cutlery, and musical instruments – which we take back to the prison and place outside as a warning to other inmates who might be considering the same thing." Another laugh. "It's been years since the last time we added someone's bones to our collection. As deterrents go, Skinny Man Row has been quite a success."

As they spoke, Lil and Lom escorted Curt and Ezra from the ready room. Holo-signs in the corridor pointed the way to customs and the adjacent tram station. Since Curt and Ezra were there on official IPF business, they weren't required to present themselves to customs inspectors, and Lil explained that a non-public tram line had been built to take scientists and government officials straight to the Slingshot research lab, located two miles from Bernard's Landing in one of the smaller domes they'd spotted from the air.

Along the way, Curt and Ezra briefed them on Starry Messenger's presumed reason for hijacking the *Titan King* and using it to take control of Cold Hell, at least so far as they knew or could reasonably surmise. Curt had just finished telling Lil that they strongly suspected the Black Pirate was actually Ul Quorn when they reached the tram station.

A small crowd of people – mainly kuiperians, but also a number of terrans, selenites, aresians, and jovians – were waiting to board the next tram to the main habitat. Instead, Lil and her lieutenant led Curt and Ezra to another part of the station, where they stopped at an unmarked door. Lil's keycard and retina scan unlocked the door, and she led the others down a short tunnel to a separate and smaller tram station, vacant save for a solitary kuiperian guard in an IPF uniform. A sleek tram car rested on its monorail by the platform, its transparent canopy already open.

"Here's where I'll leave you," Livereating Lil said, stepping aside as they gestured to the empty tram. "Vega will take you the rest of the way. The trams will accept his ID card and retina scan."

"You're not going with us?" Curt asked.

"Not necessary for me to come along, and I'm needed back here." She looked at Ezra. "'A cop's work is never done.' I think I remember someone telling me that once, way back when."

"Damn straight." Ezra gave her a wink and smile. "And I'd say you learned your lessons right well."

Lil responded with another toothy grin. A shudder went down Curt's back; he would never get used to that. He was about to board the tram when another thought occurred to him.

"If anything goes wrong," he said to Lil and Lom, "or if you don't hear anything from us in an hour, I want you to send a message to IPF HQ. Transmit it as a triple-zero priority direct to Commandant Anders, and tell him that we require Navy assistance. Can you do that?"

The smile disappeared from Lil's bearded face; she gave him a solemn nod. "One hour, then we call for military assistance. Got it, no problem." Again, Livereating Lil clasped Curt's hands within her own. "Good luck, Captain…and again, it's an honor to meet and serve with you."

The tram ride was fast, the maglev car carrying them to the Slingshot lab in just a few minutes, never coming aboveground. Lom Vega sat alone in the forward seat; he was quiet the entire trip, speaking only to the transit system AI when it requested proper identification before permitting the car to leave the station. The tall aresian seemed a little nervous, but Curt figured that it was because of the gravity of the mission. Or perhaps it was because he was in the company of Captain Future. Over the years, Curt occasionally provoked a speechless reaction in people, even fellow lawmen. No wonder Lt. Vega was quiet. As Lil said, no problem.

But Curt was wrong. There **was** a problem, and he learned what it was less than a minute after the maglev car reached its destination.

The tram ended at a small tunnel-like station, excavated from native rock deep underground, dimly lit by glowtubes in the ceiling. Curt and Ezra clumsily pried themselves out of the cramped little car and followed Lom down a narrow tunnel, which ended a short distance away at a solid-looking sphincter door. Lom Vega was leading to the door when a voice spoke up from behind them.

"So, Curt…we meet again, don't we?"

Startled, Curt turned about. There behind them stood Ul Quorn, the Magician of Mars.

XVIII

As the *Comet* settled upon its landing gear, Otho shut down the VTOL engines. There was a high, thin whine as the turbines spun down, fading in silence. A quiet stillness fell upon the ship.

To Joan, it seemed almost as if the *Comet* itself was nervous, wondering what would come next. But she knew that she was only projecting her emotions onto an inanimate object. If anyone aboard was anxious, it was she herself.

"Well," she murmured, "now what?"

Through the cockpit windows, they saw that the landing field was deserted. It was afternoon on this side of Pluto; the wan and distant sun cast anemic shadows across the stark off-white landscape; the wind picked up a handful of granular ice and spun it about, creating a miniature frost-devil. In the far distance beyond the prison, the mountains loomed upon the western horizon.

Otho's hands roamed across the pilot-side control panels. "I'm powering down the main systems, but keeping them on standby in case we need to make a quick getaway." He glanced at Joan. "Go below and suit up. I'll be down in a sec."

"Perhaps I should remain aboard," Simon said, impellers purring softly as he floated out of his alcove. "If I stay here, I can get the ship aloft that much faster."

Otho shook his head. "No, they were pretty specific about wanting everyone out where they can see us. My absence and Grag's is suspicious enough. If all three of us are missing, then they're going to be even more suspicious. They might not give up their hostages."

"All we want is Captain Lamont," Joan said as she unbuckled her seat harness and stood up. "They can keep Corvo."

"Yeah, well ..." Otho shrugged. "It's not like there's much love lost between Ul Quorn and Corvo. Maybe he just wants to get rid of the old man." He looked at the Brain. "Go with her, Simon. She'll help into your EVA body. That'll keep you alive outside."

Simon Wright followed Joan as she climbed down the ladder to the lower deck. Grag was still standing watch outside the cabin where Ashi Lanyr was being detained. On the other side of the compartment, Eek was curled up in his dog nest, napping with his head pillowed against Oog, who'd taken the form of a Persian cat.

Joan paused in front of the cabin door. "Has she said anything lately?" she asked the robot.

"Not a word," Grag said. "I think she's asleep."

"Good," Simon said, impeller whirring softly as he paused mid-air behind Joan. "Sorry to leave you behind again, but we'll need you to stay aboard and keep an eye on her."

"Wilco." Grag's head turned toward the hatch leading to the adjacent airlock and ready-room, then he looked at Joan again. "Need a hand getting Simon into his EVA body? It can be tricky."

"Yeah, that would be great," she said. "Thanks."

Grag and the Brain followed her through the hatch into the ready-room. Two EE hardsuits hung within their racks, one for her and the other for Otho. Between them hung what appeared to be another cyborg like Simon Wright, only larger and more robust, with bigger claw-manipulator and small reaction-control cluster-jets instead of impellers for mobility.

This was Simon's other body, designed specifically for use in airless or extreme environments. With Grag's help, Joan opened its clamshell-like upper carapace, revealing a circular cavity. Once Simon had settled down on the floor, he powered down his primary body, then silently and patiently waited while Joan opened it and disconnected the transparent cell in which his brain floated in a broth of life-sustaining nutrients. As soon as she was done, Grag lifted the cell, carefully carried it over to the EVA body, and gently lowered it into place.

As she connected Simon's brain with his second body, Joan pondered Otho's comment about Ul Quorn and Victor Corvo. If there was anyone the Magician of Mars despised more than Curt Newton, it was his own father. Before he turned to politics, Corvo had as his mistress a young aresian woman who'd eventually given him a son. Corvo disowned Ul Quorn as soon as he was born, though, and had his mother killed in an effort to cover up the inconvenient truth of the boy's existence. The woman's family secretly adopted the infant and raised the mixed-race orphan as one of their own, letting him know who his father was once he was old enough to understand.

When Ul Quorn reached adulthood, he reconnected with his father, now a respected member of the Solar Coalition Senate, and used that secret as leverage. In time, Ul Quorn became the aresian crime lord known as the Magician of Mars. He managed this in large part because of Corvo's power and influence, yet the son had nothing but hatred and contempt for the father.

And how did Victor Corvo feel about his son? If the former senator had any sense, he'd be scared to death that Ul Quorn might eventually reappear in his life. Even though Corvo was locked away in the toughest prison in the system, nothing could save him from the head of one of the system's most powerful gangs, a man who'd earned his nickname through a reputation for making his rivals and enemies disappear without a trace.

Hearing footsteps on the other side of the hatch leading to the passenger compartment, Joan looked around to see Otho coming in. Again, it startled her to see someone who looked exactly like Curt, whom she knew to be miles away.

"Hey, spoon-face, you done there yet?" Otho asked, addressing Grag in his own voice. "We're on the clock here."

"You know how to read a clock?" Grag asked. "If you don't, just let me know. It's easy."

Joan ignored them as she gazed past Otho at Cabin Four, visible through the open passenger-compartment hatch. The cabin door was securely locked; there was no way she could leave without someone outside letting her out. And Grag was staying behind to keep an eye on her. So there was nothing to worry about…

Or so she hoped.

XIX

When Curt took Ashi aboard the *Comet* and locked her in a cabin, he neglected something that he of all people should have remembered. Before she joined Starry Messenger, Ashi Lanyr was a professional thief, one of the best in the system. Which meant that not only was she an expert at breaking into places, she was also adept at breaking **out** of them.

If Joan, Otho or the Brain had looked in on Ashi one last time before suiting up, they would have seen something puzzling. The young woman was no longer fully dressed, but instead stripped down to her underwear. She now lay upon the bunk, blanket pulled up to her neck for warmth, eyes closed and hands folded across her breast. The one-piece bodysuit she'd been wearing was neatly folded at her feet, her mocs neatly placed beside the bed. She appeared to be taking a nap, as Grag said she was; if anyone had checked on her, that's what she would have pretended to be doing.

But she wasn't sleeping. She was listening.

Ashi overheard the brief conversation Joan had with Grag outside her cabin. It ended when they moved away from the door. Grag's heavy footsteps were easy to hear, so it wasn't hard to determine that the robot had followed Curt's new girlfriend – Ashi was disappointed to find that her old beau had taken up with an IPF officer – to the ready-room. The cyborg they called the Brain followed them; a few minutes later, she heard the android Otho come down the ladder and cross the deck. It was hard to tell which of those two creeped her out more, so she was relieved that neither of them visited her. A few moments passed, then she heard the sound she'd been anticipating, the metallic bang of the ready-room hatch slamming shut.

The instant she heard this, Ashi sprang into action.

Curt had taken the obvious precaution of searching her for weapons or anything else she might use to help her escape. He'd done this even before the *Comet* departed Stratos Venera. However, although he'd had her remove the skinsuit she'd been wearing, chivalry had stopped him from demanding that she submit to a strip-search. Besides, the bodysuit Ashi wore beneath the vacuum gear was skin-tight; she couldn't have concealed any weapons without them being visible. Even the lightweight mocs she'd worn inside her boots were little more than socks with treaded rubber soles. So Curt was certain that Ashi wasn't hiding a stunner or a set of lock picks, and therefore he was certain that, once he locked her in Cabin 4 aboard the *Comet,* she'd stay there until he, Joan, or one of the Futuremen let her out.

If he'd made her remove her bodysuit and mocs, too, and given them a close inspection, he wouldn't have been so confident.

Sitting up on the bunk, Ashi bent down and picked up her clothes. She placed the mocs beside her, then went to work on the bodysuit. Turning the one-piece garment upside down and inside out, she lifted the ankle of the suit's right leg, located the stitch-work of its inseam, and bit into it with her front teeth.

It took a little gnawing, but Ashi finally managed to rip open the seam with her teeth. Revealed was something resembling a thin white ribbon sewn into the suit's lining. Ashi carefully tore open the inseam all the way to the crotch. As a garment, the bodysuit was ruined and unwearable, but it hardly mattered; concealed within its right leg was a 24-inch length of ribbon-like cord.

Ashi went to the cabin door and knelt beside it. Delicately, she peeled away the cord's cellophane backing, exposing its adhesive inner surface. She affixed the ribbon to the door's recessed handle and thumbplate, making sure that it completely covered the lock.

She worked carefully but fast. She didn't know how long Grag would be away from his post outside her door, and she'd already learned that the robot's hearing was better than a human's and he could pick up even the softest of sounds inside her cabin. But Ashi accomplished the task before Grag returned from helping Joan and the Brain into their gear. Once the det cord was in place, she picked up her mocs and went to work on them.

She tore off the sole of the left moccasin. Concealed within it was a coiled length of insulated electric wire, not much thicker than a hair but nonetheless capable of carrying a 9v current, and a wafer-thin detonator powered by a tiny battery. Working with practiced precision, Ashi connected the wire to the detonator, then spliced the other end to the det cord.

She'd just made sure all the connections were firm when she heard the ready-room hatch open again. Grag's heavy footsteps signaled the robot's return. Ashi silently cursed. She had one more thing to do, and it was possible that the 'bot might hear her before she was ready.

Grag didn't immediately come back to where he'd been standing outside her cabin, though, instead walking a few feet from the hatch and halting. This mystified her for a moment or two until she recalled the layout of the compartment. The 'bot had walked over to the port-side porthole. No sooner had she realized this when her ears picked up a couple of faint thumps: the main airlock's outer hatch opening and the gangway ladder unfolding. Now it all made sense: Grag had gone over to where he could watch Joan, Otho and the Brain exit the *Comet* and come down the ladder. Which put him just far enough from her cabin that, so long as she was quiet, he couldn't hear her through the door.

Quickly and silently, Ashi picked up the other moccasin and peeled off its sole. Hidden within a small compartment in the arch was a flat, rectangular device with two recessed buttons on one side, marked *Off* and *Reset*. Stamped on the other side of its plastic case was the stylized logo of a familiar brand-name, Grag Robotics.

This was the Indiana-based company that built Grag. When the robot developed a consciousness and personality atypical of a construction robot, Grag had taken the name of his creator as his own. But while Grag demanded to be treated like a human, the fact remained that he was still a robot. And because robots had been known to malfunction and pose a threat to humans, they were sold with a safeguard: a wireless remote complete with a kill switch, capable of instantly shutting down a 'bot that had run amok.

Ashi held in her hands a remote for Grag's make and model. She patiently waited until she heard Grag leave the porthole and walk back across the compartment. As soon as the robot halted outside her door, she pressed the *Off* button.

A sharp series of beeps from outside told her that Grag was now unconscious, inert, and unable to do anything to stop her. Ashi kissed the remote and tossed it on the bunk, then picked up the detonator. Crouching behind the bunk, she took a deep breath and pushed the button.

There was a loud **bang!** as door lock was exploded by the shaped charge. By then, Joan, Otho and the Brain had exited the ship and had climbed down the ladder; they heard nothing. There was now a smoking hole where the handle and touchdown had once been. The door slid open easily, and Ashi stepped out into the lower-deck living area, clutching her blanket around her for warmth.

Grag stood nearby, arms at his side, massive head slumped forward on his neck. He looked like a man who'd literally fallen asleep on his feet. He didn't move as Ashi walked around behind him. Closely inspecting his back, she located a small service panel. Ashi slid it open and pushed a button located within. A sharp double-beep, and she closed the panel again. There: the 'bot was completely shut down, and wouldn't power-up again until someone came along and reversed the procedure she'd just done.

Pulling the blanket around her near-naked body, Ashi crossed the compartment and opened the hatch to the ready-room. In three steps she was at the airlock. The inner hatch was shut, and a quick peek through its small porthole confirmed that the chamber was vacant, its outer door still open.

Despite the chill that raised goosebumps across her body, there was a satisfied smile on Ashi's face. Rubbing her arms beneath the blanket, she hastily went to a utility locker she'd spotted when she'd come aboard the *Comet*. Opening it, she found what she hoped it would contain, a spare wireless headset. She fit it upon her head, then switched it to the channel she knew was being monitored and adjusted the mic wand.

"Ghost One to Liberator Two," she said, trying hard to keep her teeth from chattering. "Do you copy? Over."

A moment passed, then Gray Garson's voice came over. "We copy, Ghost One. Do you have control of Big C? Over."

"Not yet, Liberator Two. The Futuremen have just exited the ship and the robot has been disabled. Will report soon. Over."

Without waiting for a response, Ashi returned to the airlock. Although she couldn't enter it while the outside hatch remained open, nonetheless she was able to operate it through the control panel on the bulkhead beside the inside hatch. Flipping open its panel, she found the button that closed the outer hatch and pushed it.

The outer hatch closed quickly. The moment it was shut and sealed tight, Ashi activated the pressurization cycle. A bar-indicator above the hatch began to move from red to green. When it reached green, the airlock was fully pressurized and locked from the inside. Since the airlock's safety features would prevent anyone outside from entering the *Comet* without someone inside depressurizing it first, the Futuremen were effectively locked out of their own ship.

"Liberator Two, this is Ghost One," she said, trying to keep the excitement she felt out of her voice. "I have control of the *Comet*. Repeat...I have control of the *Comet*. Over."

"Excellent, Ghost One! Well done!" Judging from the background sound of cheering men, Ashi figured that Garson wasn't alone and other men had heard her. "Remain there until we're ready to come over, and don't open the airlock before you hear from us. Over."

"Wilco. Ghost One over and out." Ashi muted the headset but left it active, then hurried out of the ready room. Her clothes were ruined, but she was positive she could find something to wear in Joan's quarters. It had probably been many years since the last time many of the men in Cold Hell had seen a woman; better put something on before they got there.

If Ashi had any pangs of a compromised conscience about what she'd done, they were gone by the time she was dressed again. This was the second occasion she'd betrayed Curt; this time was easier than the first.

XX

The moment he laid eyes on Ul Quorn, Curt made a grab for the plasma pistol holstered at his hip. Ezra had the same reaction; for him, it was the PBP he carried. But their hands didn't come within an inch of their weapons before Ul Quorn raised his own particle beam pistol.

"Uh-uh," he said. "I wouldn't do that if I were you."

Curt froze. From the corner of his eye, he saw a half-dozen men and women step in sight. Too late, he noticed a door on the right side of the tunnel he, Ezra, and Lom Vega had just walked down; it was marked STORAGE 2, just the sort of thing the eye flits across without taking note of. Obviously, they'd been hiding within the storage closet, awaiting Curt's arrival. Judging from the orange prison jumpsuits most of them wore, many of Ul Quorn's gang were Cold Hell inmates.

"If Captain Future suddenly disappears," Ul Quorn added, speaking to them, "aim for the place where he's now standing, and also to the right and left of it. He can become invisible, but he can't teleport." The half-aresian, half-terran crimelord gave Curt a knowing smile. "You've played that trick before, remember? You can fool me, but not twice."

Curt and Ezra exchanged a silent glance as they raised their hands. Curt wasn't wearing his personal fantomas generator; the drawback of using it was that, once it was activated, its field deflected all light rays, including those entering his eyes; therefore, he became blind. That impediment made him reluctant to wear it all the time. So becoming invisible wasn't an option. Ezra knew that but Ul Quorn didn't, and Curt saw no reason to tell him otherwise. Still, he wished he'd had the foresight to wear it today.

"Wouldn't dream of it," Curt said dryly. "And I take it you survived our encounter by jumping down a volcano shaft, yes?"

"Oh, so you figured that out, did you?" It was hard to tell whether the disappointed frown on Ul Quorn's face was genuine or mockery. "I assumed you had. You're rather intelligent...or so I thought until now." He glanced at the inmates standing nearest to Curt and Ezra. "Take their weapons, please."

"Is that why you pretended to be the Black Pirate?" Curt asked.

"Yeah, what's with that, anyway?" Ezra scowled at the former inmate who approached him to take his gun. "Careful there, boy. I'm a mite particular 'bout who puts his mitts on my shootin' iron."

The inmate hesitated; the stone-cold look in Ezra's eyes was sufficient to make him take the old lawman seriously. "Take his gun," Ul Quorn commanded his henchman. "If he touches you, I'll vaporize his head." To underscore his threat, he raised his PBP and took a dead bead on Ezra's face. "I have reasons to keep Curt alive, Marshal Gurney, but you're expendable. Don't do anything you won't live to regret."

"Do as he says," Curt murmured. Ezra glared at the inmate, but didn't move a muscle as the young terran carefully came forward to pluck the PBP from his belt. "The question stands," Curt continued, forcing himself to relax while another inmate took the plasma gun from his holster and detached its cable from the power unit on his belt. There was no other gun like it; the inmate studied it for a moment, then grinned and stuck it in his pocket, not realizing that his trophy couldn't be used without external power. "Why the whole 'Black Pirate' charade?" Curt went on. "You're not wearing the outfit any more, I notice."

Indeed, the Black Pirate's skintight black suit with its matching cape and cowl were gone. Instead, Ul Quorn wore kuiperian cold-weather clothes similar to the arctic survival gear of Earth's polar inhabitants, even though some of it seemed a little small for his tall frame.

Ul Quorn hesitated, quietly regarding his captives as if trying to decide how much to tell them when he didn't really need to tell them anything at all. Curt patiently waited, and after a minute the Magician of Mars made up his mind. "I took the identity of the Black

Pirate," he began, "because if you'd known I was behind the taking of the *Liberator* –"

"The *Titan King,* you mean," Ezra interrupted.

Ul Quorn gave an exasperated sigh, then casually pointed his PGP at the marshal's feet and fired. A scarlet beam bored a hole into the concrete floor between Ezra's boots, missing his right foot by only an inch. Ezra didn't cry out, and his boots remained rooted to the spot. The marshal didn't startle easily.

Again, Ul Quorn seemed disappointed. "Don't be rude," he said, then looked at Lom Vega. "If he interrupts me again, shoot him in the knees, both of them." His eyes met Ezra's "Maybe having to get your legs remade will teach you some manners."

Lom Vega nodded, a smug smile on his face. Curt didn't need to be told that the aresian was a Starry Messenger infiltrator. He remembered Livereating Lil mentioning the fact that the IPF had sent Lom to Pluto just four months ago. Apparently this was part of Ul Quorn's plan, too. He was putting something in motion…but what?

Ezra didn't respond except to glare at the turncoat IPF officer. Ul Quorn returned his attention to Curt. "If you'd known I was responsible for the *Liberator* takeover or the prison uprising, then you would've reacted differently. Maybe brought the entire SolCol Navy with you. But since everything was predicated on luring you here from Venus –"

"What?" Curt stared at him. Ezra's mouth fell open, but he wisely chose silence.

"Oh really," Ul Quorn said, "you must have realized by now that the bomb Ashi planted on the Stratos Venera rotorvator was a fake." Another glance at Ezra. "IPF's intelligence was good, Marshal Gurney, but the reason why your informants heard about the plot in the first place was because we **wanted** them to know about it." He looked at Curt again. "You see now? The entire purpose of that little act was to get Ashi aboard your ship."

"We were wondering about that," Curt admitted.

"Then perhaps it's also occurred to you that it's no coincidence that, at the very same time the Starry Messenger cell on Venera Stratos was conducting its action, the *Liberator* reached Pluto and we were instigating the prison uprising." Ul Quorn's right eyebrow arched. "No? Then I also take it that you haven't studied the respective orbital positions of Venus, Saturn, and Pluto. They're currently in conjunction on the same side of the system, with only thirty AU's separating Saturn from Pluto."

"I wouldn't exactly call that close."

"Close enough for...well, I'm getting ahead of myself. Before I go any further, I need to check something." Holstering his pistol, Ul Quorn prodded the comlink inserted in his right ear. "Liberator Two, this is Liberator One. Report ... over."

Curt couldn't hear what Liberator Two was saying; his Anni wasn't linked to the radio frequency Ul Quorn was using. So he had to wait while Ul Quorn listened to his operative and hope that the other person wasn't at Cold Hell. But even that faint hope was dashed as a wily grin spread across the crimelord's face.

"Yes, we've captured Captain Future," Ul Quorn said after a few moments. "The **real** Captain Future. The one you got, that's the android. He's in disguise." A brief pause. "Uh-huh, yeah. That's what I thought he'd do...didn't I tell you? Hold on a sec." He tapped the comlink to mute it, then shook his head and chuckled as he looked at Curt again. "A word to the wise, sir...never attempt the same trick twice."

Curt didn't reply, but his face burned. This wasn't the first time Otho had disguised himself to look like Curt so that Captain Future could be in two places at once. They had used it when he and the Futuremen had gone up against Gray Garson. Ul Quorn must have learned about this gag from Garson, who'd been sentenced to Cold Hell after Captain Future brought him to justice. This meant that Garson had teamed up with Ul Quorn and his gang after they took over the prison. No telling how many others whom he'd gone up against in the past had done so, too.

Curt remained stoical, but inside he was kicking himself. Damn it, he'd underestimated Ul Quorn. This wasn't an ordinary Starry Messenger plot; their leader was playing a more complex game than he and the Futuremen had anticipated.

Ul Quorn was listening to his comlink again. "Yes…all right…excellent! Put them in position, then go to standby on this channel and be ready to switch to video. Over." He muted the comlink again, then looked at Lom Vega. "Open the door, please." As the aresian stepped to the vault door leading to the lab, Ul Quorn turned to his men. "Lead them in. And don't let them out of your sight for a moment." He cocked his head at Curt. "Especially him. He's got the luck of the devil."

"I could say the same of you," Curt said. "Particularly the devil part."

"Naw, he ain't the devil," Ezra said, shaking his head. "But I surely wish he'd go to him."

"My, aren't we clever?" Ul Quorn snorted in disgust. "Marshal, really…"

He was interrupted by the digital beep of a code number being entered into a pinpad, followed by the faint whirr of a biometric scanner analyzing Lom's face and verifying his identity. A loud snap of recessed locks sliding back, then the renegade IPF officer grasped the locklever with both hands, twisted it clockwise, and swung open the heavy portal.

"Welcome, Magician of Mars," Lom Vega said, bowing to Ul Quorn before the open door. "Your prize awaits."

Like a conquistador striding into a conquered city, Ul Quorn marched into the secret lab. His men prodded Curt and Ezra to follow him. As they did, what they saw on the other side of the door took Curt's breath away.

They entered an enormous chamber about a hundred feet in diameter, excavated from native rock and with a barrel ceiling high above a polished black-marble floor. The walls were crowded with all manner of scientific instruments: computer workstations, lab benches, precision lasers and microwave lathes, an electron microscope, a vacuum cell containing the cryogenic capsule of a quantum AI. But it was the object at the center of the room that drew Curt's attention.

Half-enclosed by a scaffold, a giant cylinder lay on its side. About twenty feet wide by sixty feet long, flat at one end and tapering at the other, the cylinder was constructed of stainless steel burnished to a reflective finish. Eight concentric hoops encircled it, connected to the cylinder by slender spars. Inspection ports and instrument panels were scattered across both sides; power and data-relay cables snaked across the floor to nearby control podiums.

Slingshot. Without asking, Curt knew at once this was what it was. An engine designed by alien technology and derived from plans carved into the petroglyphs left behind by Denebian explorers a million years ago. The means to open a gateway to the other side of the galaxy ...

And now Ul Quorn had it. But to what purpose?

"You are in charge, yes? Then you have what you want! Release my people!"

Curt looked around, searching for the source of the querulous voice with a thick aresian accent. On the other side of the lab, a handful of men and women of different races were squatting or kneeling on the floor, hands planted atop their heads. It wasn't hard to tell that they were scientists and technicians; they wore white lab jumpsuits, ID and radiation badges clipped to their chests. They were guarded by more of Ul Quorn's recruits, carrying guns they'd taken from the prison. Curt wondered how they'd gotten into the lab ahead of Ul Quorn if the door was locked from inside.

The scientist who'd spoken up was a middle-aged aresian, his dark hair and beard streaked with gray, his dark eyes angry. "Excuse me a moment," Ul Quorn said to Curt, then he strode over to the prisoners. "Ah! You must be Slingshot Project's chief scientist...Tiko Thrinn, am I right?"

"I am Dr. Tiko," the scientist snapped, undaunted by the particle beam rifle prodding the back of his neck. "And just who the hell are you?"

"Ul Quorn, the Magician of Mars." The crimelord placed his hands on his hips and preened, confident of his infamy. "As a fellow aresian, I'm sure my reputation precedes me."

"Never heard of you," Tiko Thrinn snapped, "and furthermore I couldn't give a damn if you were Sarge Saturn. **Get out of my goddamn lab!**"

Despite themselves, the other scientists on either side of him broke out in laughter. "You tell 'em, Thrinn," said a selenite lab tech, grinning with amusement. "He's –"

Ul Quorn yanked the PGP from his holster, leveled it at the technician, and squeezed the trigger. The selenite collapsed, a thumb-size hole burned through his chest. The others screamed in terror as he fell upon the floor, arms and legs twitching as he died. Only Tiko Thrinn remained silent, although there was vengeful rage in his eyes.

Ul Quorn holstered his pistol again and looked at the bearded jovian standing behind them. Curt noticed that he wore the remnants of a *Titan King* uniform, its insignia removed. "Next person who laughs or speaks without permission, Harl, do the same," Ul Quorn said, "Except for Dr. Tiko. His survival is necessary…for the time being, at least."

Tiko Thrinn glared at Ul Quorn but kept his thoughts to himself. Ul Quorn let out his breath, then looked around at Curt. "How rude," he murmured, his tone apologetic. Then, apparently wishing to change the subject, he forced a smile. "I bet you're wondering how Harl and his people got here before we did. Well, it's simple. I had a hunch that there might be another way for people to enter the lab besides through the front door, so I asked Lom Vega if he'd investigate. And sure enough, he discovered that there is…an underground maglev, leading straight from Cold Hell. The prison uses it as a fast way of sending supplies here. And not only that, but the airlock at this end wasn't even locked. So as soon as we had control of the prison, I sent my associates Harl al-Sarakka and Athor Az here to take over the lab while I came by ice crawler to the front entrance to meet you."

He waited for Curt to say something. Wanting to avoid further bloodshed, Curt said, "Smart, very smart." Ul Quorn chuckled and took a mocking bow. "But there's still something you haven't told me. Why go to all this trouble to get me here? Do you want revenge that badly?"

Ul Quorn stared at him, mouth falling open in surprise. At first, it seemed as if he was about to laugh again. Instead, he merely shook his head. "No, you misunderstand. My motives don't include vengeance against you and your crew. In fact, I couldn't really care less whether you're here or not. It's not **you** I want…it's something you **have**."

He stopped, waiting for Curt to put it together. Curt looked at Ul Quorn, then Tiko Thrinn, then the prototype wormhole generator behind them. And suddenly he understood.

"No, it's not me," he said. "It's never been me. You want the *Comet.*"

XXI

Joan realized that she and the others had walked into a trap the moment she set foot inside Cold Hell. Unfortunately, that revelation came a moment too late.

There was no one on the landing field when she and the Futuremen climbed down the *Comet*'s portside ladder. A few moments passed, then a voice came through their helmet headsets, instructing them to proceed to the prison's main entrance, and warning them again to leave behind any weapons they might be carrying.

So Joan, Otho and Ezra walked up the frozen path to Cold Hell, Simon silently floating along behind them in his enhanced cyborg body. The only party to greet them was Skinny Man Row, the skeletons crucified just outside the prison walls. A sheer wall of rock-hard ice loomed above them; an airlock was located at its base, its outer door already open.

Something about the absence of any living person besides themselves made Joan uneasy. If there had been just one person waiting to meet them, it wouldn't have been as sinister as finding no one at all. When she hesitated, though, the voice repeated its demand, more forcefully this time.

She turned to look at Otho. She could see his face clearly through his helmet faceplate, and the android looked so much like Curt that, for a moment, she forgot that he wasn't here but many miles away. Although he wore Captain Future's face, there was little reassuring about his expression. The Curt Newton she knew would've come up with something, maybe a wisecrack, to relax her; Otho was good at **looking** like Curt, but **being** Curt was another matter entirely. They couldn't even engage in a silent conversation via virtual telepathy; Cold Hell's Anni-dampening field interfered with their neural-net implants.

All they could do was give each other a silent nod, then step through the door into the airlock, with Grag shutting and sealing the door behind them.

It didn't take long for the airlock to pressurize. When the cycle was finished, the control panel chimed to let Joan and Otho know that it was okay to enter the ready-room, but no sooner had they left the airlock than the unseen voice addressed them again. "Please remove your suits, but don't exit until someone opens the inner hatch. Follow our instructions and don't do anything stupid. You are being observed at all times."

"No kidding," Otho muttered. "I never would've guessed."

"And I'm sure they're listening to us, too," Joan added. An obvious warning, but she felt like she had to say something to remind Otho not to use his own voice when he spoke. To underline this, she added, "When you have a chance, would you help me with this suit…Curt?"

Otho gave her a sharp look. They were usually careful to avoid addressing Curt as anything but Captain Future while out in public. "Of course, Joan," he replied, and gave her a furtive wink. Message received and understood.

It took almost ten minutes for Joan and Otho to climb out of their EE gear; without Grag's assistance, and the Brain unable to give them much help, the procedure took somewhat longer. When they were finally done, Joan and Otho dragged the suits over to the other side of the room where other EE gear was suspended within suit racks. Joan noticed that several racks were empty, indicating that someone had recently left through the prison's main airlock. If that were true, why didn't they spot anyone outside?

It was then she realized that she, Otho and Simon had been snared. Whatever happened next, it wasn't likely to be a simple matter of negotiating the release of hostages. For now, though, they had little choice but to wait and see.

As it turned out, they were kept waiting longer than expected. Almost half an hour went by, during which no one spoke to them again through the comlink. There was a small round window in the door, but someone had opaqued it with a sheet of brown paper, and although the ready-room was heated, the room was still cold enough that Joan could see her breath when she exhaled. Fortunately, she and Otho had thought to wear insulated jumpsuits beneath their EE gear, so at least they weren't going to freeze to death…just die of boredom.

Joan was considering the risks of forcing open the door when it made a loud click. "All right, come out," the voice growled as it swung open, not through the comlink but from just outside. "Keep your hands where we can see them and don't get cute."

Otho silently motioned for her to step out first. Damn it, he was being gallant as always, but he was forgetting the role he was playing. "After you, chief," she said, subtly reminded Otho that, as Captain Future, he should be the one to go first. Hoping that no one noticed his hesitation, Joan followed him, with Simon whirring behind her.

They found themselves in a large, enclosed space resembling an indoor courtyard, with a broad skylight window high overhead. Tiered second- and third-floor balconies overlooked carefully tended gardens and benches; the air was warm, and the shallow light of the distant sun was augmented by solar collectors arrayed outside the pressure-resistant panes of the skylight. Obviously an exercise yard that had been given over to the inmates, who'd transformed this part of Cold Hell into an atrium not unlike the commons of a small town on Earth.

It might have actually been pleasant if it wasn't part of a penitentiary. The resemblance ended at the hatch they'd just come through, where an electrified steel-mesh grate had been deactivated and rolled aside. Glancing up at the third-floor balconies, Joan saw that they were also protected by grates; they served as a sentry platform. A dead Jovian wearing an IPF uniform lay sprawled upon the half-open grate of one of the platforms, a silent testament to just how rapidly the uprising had occurred and the guards had been wiped out.

The commons was crowded with inmates. So far as Joan could tell, nearly all of them were armed with particle beam pistols, assault rifles, batons, and riot gear taken from murdered guards or lifted from the prison armory. She'd never seen so many guns. The fact that the three of them were unarmed did nothing for her peace of mind. A small area directly in front of the airlock had been cleared, with the closest inmates forming a semi-circle around them.

The crowd parted to let someone through, a terran she'd never expected to see again: Grey Garson, the former space-industrialist whom she and Curt had exposed as the perpetrator of acts of deep-space sabotage against ships belonging to corporate rivals, some costing the lives of many spacers. Captain Future and the Futuremen, along with her and Ezra, had brought Garson's ring to justice; Garson alone had survived, and a Lunar Republic judge on the Moon had sentenced him to life in Cold Hell. The last time Joan had seen Garson, he was being led out of the Descartes City courtroom. As he walked by, Garson had given her a sly wink, quietly reminding her that, until she and Curt discovered his role, she'd found him rather attractive.

"Hello, Joan," Garson said, his tone as unctuous as it had been in the courtroom. "A pleasure to see you again." He winked at her; she responded with a dark scowl that made it disappear. If Garson had known what she was thinking, he would've been relieved that Lt. Randall wasn't presently armed.

Garson looked as if he was about to add something, then clasped a hand against his earpiece. Turning his back to Joan, he had a brief discussion with someone. Probably Ul Quorn himself, she guessed. While this was going on, Simon floated a little closer to her and Otho.

"We're in a jam," the Brain said quietly, "but we've been in worse situations. Just don't give –"

"Shaddup, you freak." One of the inmates, a terran whose face and shaved skull were covered with tattoos, reversed the rifle in his hands and slammed its stock against the back of Simon's carapace. The Brain wasn't damaged, but his eyestalks twisted about to transfix his assailant with a stare.

"The last person to do that to me," Simon said, "is still trying to find his face after I peeled it off and threw it away." He raised his claws menacingly. Suddenly nervous, the inmate involuntarily stepped back.

Observing this, Joan smiled despite herself. Even outnumbered and surrounded, criminals throughout the system knew better than to mess with the Futuremen. And she had little doubt that Curt would save them.

However, her hopes that Captain Future would ride to the rescue were soon dashed. Putting Ul Quorn on hold, Grey Garson turned to his prisoners. He regarded the three of them with contempt for a few moments before walking over to Otho.

"Take off that stupid disguise," he said. "You're not him." Before Otho could react, Garson grabbed a fistful of red hair atop the android's head and yanked. The wig made a faint ripping sound as it tore loose from his head, exposing Otho's bald white pate. "You disgust me," Garson muttered, tossing the wig to the floor. "Captain Future, at least I can respect, but you…"

"'The opprobrium of assholes is a badge of honor,'" Otho responded, quoting 20th century author Norman Spinrad. A bit crude, but it got the point across.

Garson glared at him, then the smirk reappeared. Reaching into the thigh pocket of his prison jumpsuit, he pulled out a discus-like portable holo projector. "Bring the hostages up here," he said to no one in particular as he bent over to place the projector on the floor before Joan, Otho and the Brain. "Let's get everyone in on this, shall we?"

Garson switched on the projector, and a shimmering translucent image formed in midair above it: Curt and Ezra, one-third life-size, each with their hands locked together atop their heads. Garson pulled a remote from his other pocket, pointed it at his own prisoners, and pushed a button. The projector immediately cast a cone of pale yellow around Otho, the Brain and Joan; judging from the way Curt and Ezra suddenly looked off to one side, it was clear that they could see holos of their companions as well.

"The gang's all here," Curt said drily. "Anyone got a deck of cards?"

"How droll," Ul Quorn said. At first, they could only hear his voice, then the Starry Messenger leader stepped within range of the holo projector. It startled Joan to see the Black Pirate unmasked. "But if it's a game you want," he went on, "I've got one for you."

As he spoke, as if on cue, two men were pulled through the crowd and thrust in beside Joan, Otho and Simon. One wore the uniform of a spaceliner's commanding officer; Joan assumed he was Captain Henri Lamont of the *Titan King*. The other wore the orange jumpsuit of an inmate; he was overweight and losing his hair, and it took her a moment to recognize him as Victor Corvo. Prison life hadn't been kind to the former senator; he was pale with fright, and when he saw first Joan and the Futuremen, and then the holo projections of Curt and Ezra, his eyes went wide.

"Oh my god," he said, his voice cracking with fear, "you captured them, too." He turned his head to look at Ul Quorn's image. "Look, son...you got your ransom, you got Newton and his bunch, you've even managed to liberate the entire prison. What more do you want? Just let me go and I'll –"

"You think I give a damn about ransom, or even you?" Ul Quorn laughed at his father. "No, that's not why I'm here. I have a much bigger game in mind...and Gray was right, this is a game." Turning away from Corvo's holo-image, he looked at Curt. "All right, here are the rules. In fact, there's just one. Now that I've got the *Comet* –"

"I don't believe you," Curt said. "You're a liar."

"No, Curt, it's true," Joan interjected. "The whole thing was a set-up. They tricked us into taking Ashi aboard the ship and bringing her here, then they tricked us again by luring us off the ship while leaving her there."

She felt her face becoming warm. "Grag is still aboard," she went on, "but somehow she's managed to shut him down, then lock us out. So it's just as he says...he's got control of the *Comet*." She let out her breath and shook her head. "I'm sorry, Curt. I messed up."

"**We** messed up," Curt said. "It's my fault, too." His gaze shifted to Ul Quorn. "All right, Ul, you've won your little game, so – "

"Won?" Ul Quorn laughed out loud. "I haven't even started yet!" The smile disappeared. "So let's get serious, shall we?" he said as he slid a hand into the pocket of his parka and produced a PBP. "What I want you to do is take control of the *Comet*, fly it into orbit, and reconnect with its warp torus. Once this is done, you will rendezvous with the *Liberator*...the *Titan King*, if you prefer...and dock with it. A cradle has been assembled at the bow that's large enough for two additions: your ship, and also –"

"Slingshot," Curt said.

Joan's eyes widened. All of a sudden, the pieces were falling together. She now knew why Ul Quorn had gone to such lengths to get his hands on the *Comet*. The prototype spacetime-traversal device codenamed Slingshot required a source of dark energy in order to produce a stable wormhole, but the one in the lab was a test unit suitable only for experiments; it wasn't flightworthy, not having been designed for actual service. Solar Coalition Navy vessels had dark-energy generators for their Alcubierre warp drives, but the only way Ul Quorn would ever acquire one of those would be to hijack a SCN vessel...fat chance of that. And Starry Messenger simply did not have the resources to build one of their own. It was a separatist organization, not a scientific R&D group.

But the *Comet* had a warp drive almost identical to SCN vessels, having been designed and built in the Solar Coalition shipyards on the Moon. Indeed, the principal difference between the *Comet's* dark energy generator and those aboard naval spacecraft was that the former was a slightly more advanced third-generation version. And since it would be easier to hijack Captain Future's vessel than a warship with dozens of crewmembers aboard...

"Ah...now you understand." Ul Quorn nodded approvingly. "Once the Slingshot has been transported to the *Liberator* and mated with the *Comet's* warp engine, we'll be able to open a stable wormhole."

"To where?" Curt asked.

"I can answer that question," another voice said.

Because she wasn't in the Slingshot Project lab, Joan couldn't see who'd just spoken up. Yet Simon Wright recognized the voice. "Tiko Thrinn," he said, speaking softly so that the inmates guarding them wouldn't hear him. "The project leader. Brilliant man, one of the foremost physicists of our time. If they've got him, too, then they have one of the two people they'll need to interface Slingshot with the *Comet.*"

"Who's the other one?" Joan whispered.

"Guess," the Brain replied, but Joan didn't need to; she'd figured it out the moment the words slipped from her mouth.

Dr. Tiko continued to speak. "The petroglyphs left behind on Mars and the Moon by the Denebians gave detailed instructions about how to go about building a spacetime traversal device," he said to Curt, "but it's not a gateway to anywhere. In fact, the wormhole it'll create has just one destination...the Deneb system itself."

"You're positive about that?" Curt asked.

"Of course we're sure." There was a hint of arrogance in the physicist's voice; he was clearly a man who didn't suffer fools gladly. "Once we finished putting Slingshot together and connected it with the dark energy generator we also built, we opened a small wormhole right here in the lab and stabilized it just long enough to send a probe through. The hole collapsed about ten seconds later, but that was enough time for the probe to transmit images of what it saw before it was lost to us: a nearby planet and the star it orbited. We didn't recognize the planet, of course, but the star was a type-A supergiant, and once our computers analyzed the images, it recognized the background stars as those in Deneb's constellation as seen from Earth. In other words –"

"It's the Denebian system," Ul Quorn said, "and the planet is the Denebian homeworld."

"Yes." Tiko gave him a sour look; he clearly didn't like being interrupted, but made allowances for someone holding a gun on him. "It's a bit surprising to discover a race inhabiting a planet of a star not usually considered habitable, but apparently the Denebians are an exception."

"In any case," Ul Quorn continued, "the Denebians wanted humans to visit them once we were able to do so, which is why they left behind instructions. I determined that myself when I interpreted the lunar petroglyphs, and although I wasn't able to complete my own translation of the Martian petroglyphs, I knew that someone else would come behind me and finish my work once their existence was known. So I slipped some of my people into the Solar Coalition scientific community and patiently waited to see what they'd find, and –"

"You found out about Slingshot," Curt said. "All right, now I understand…except for one thing. What do you expect to get out of using Slingshot to reach Deneb? What's the purpose behind all this?"

For a moment, it seemed as if Ul Quorn was going to answer that question, for he opened his mouth to speak. Then he appeared to reconsider; instead, he shook his head. "No, I'm not going to tell you that," he said, favoring Curt with a sly grin. "You'll have to wait until we reach Deneb."

"We?" Curt looked at him askance. "What makes you think I'm going with you, let alone helping you at all?"

"Have you forgotten? I'm holding hostages…the Futuremen, Captain Lamont, and your friends from the IPF." He paused. "And, of course, my dear beloved father, Senator Corvo."

"**What?**" Until now, Victor Corvo had remained largely silent. Yet this was one indignity he wouldn't suffer. "Quorn, I'm not…damn it all, I'm on your side!" He waved a hand at Gray Garson. "These are my people, not yours! They don't do anything without my say-so!"

"Really? Is that a fact?" Ul Quorn's head turned slightly, as if he was in the same location as Garson and able to look him in the eye. "M'sieur Garson?" he asked, and Garson nodded. "M'sieur Garson, I'll give you a choice. You and your fellow inmates can join my people, and thereby put an end to your captivity and become soldiers in a worthy cause. Or you can remain loyal to Senator Corvo…correction, **former** Senator Corvo…and enjoy a few hours of freedom until I've kept my word, released my hostages, and departed with the *Liberator*, at which point the SolCol Navy will swoop in and put everyone back in their cages. So which will it be?"

"I think I'll join you," Garson said.

"Very good. I thought that would be your decision." Ul Quorn paused, and the smile vanished from his face as if it had never been there. "But first, I need for you to do something for me, to prove your loyalty and also to demonstrate to Captain Future my willingness to take lives if he refuses to follow my orders. I want you to kill my father."

"What?" Corvo shouted. "No! You're my –!"

"Sorry, Vic," Garson said. And then he stepped up behind Corvo, raised his PBP until its barrel nearly touched the middle of the senator's back, and blew a hole through his heart.

XXII

C orvo's murder marked the beginning of Curt's ordeal.

Ul Quorn wasted no time shedding tears for a father who'd disowned him as a child. Victor Corvo's body was unceremoniously dragged to the airlock and thrown outside; "Let the cannibals have him," his son said, as if the kuiperians were nothing more than savages who'd indiscriminately feast on any human corpse they found. He then commenced issuing orders to the prison inmates who, having seen what could happen to those who displeased him, knew that they were to be carried out without question or fail.

First, he instructed Garson to have the remaining hostages – Joan, Otho, the Brain and Henri Lamont – moved to a prison cell, with two sentry robots posted outside as guards. No harm was to come to them, he said, nor were they to be harassed or neglected in any way. The only persons permitted to visit them, though, were Garson and Ul Quorn himself, save for a couple of inmates tasked with bringing them meals.

Although Ul Quorn told his prisoners that they'd be respected "as if you're house guests," he also warned them that, if they were contemplating an escape attempt, the 'bots were instructed to shoot to kill. Having witnessed the cold-blooded way in which Victor Corvo was eliminated, Joan, Otho and the Brain knew better than to ignore the warning.

Henri Lamont remained silent. He'd spoken little since he'd been introduced to Joan and the Futuremen, and the way in which he carried himself – head down, hands at his sides, sluggishly obeying all orders – suggested a broken man. Yet Joan noticed an ember of defiance still smoldering in his eyes, the quiet way he observed every move their captors made. The *Titan King*'s captain hadn't surrendered completely. Although he said almost nothing to his cell mates, Joan quietly concluded that he'd stand with them if and when the opportunity arose.

As for Curt and Ezra, they were kept away from their companions for only a little while longer. As soon as Grey Garson was certain that matters at the prison were under control, he and Ul Quorn switched places; Garson took the underground tram from Cold Hell to the Slingshot lab, and as soon as it arrived, Ul Quorn climbed aboard and rode it back to the prison. He didn't travel alone; Curt and Ezra came with him, together with a pair of hulking jovian inmates as their guards.

Along the way, Ul Quorn briefly described the plan to Curt and Ezra. Garson's task was to oversee Slingshot's removal from the R&D lab and its transportation to orbit, where it would be mated with the *Liberator*. Captain Lamont would assist him with this, since he knew the protocols and passwords that would allow the liner's AI system to interface with Slingshot's quantum DNA computer. While this was going on, Curt and Simon would accompany Ul Quorn to the *Comet*. Once they were aboard, they'd take the ship back into space, reconnect with the warp torus, then travel to higher orbit for rendezvous and docking with the *Liberator*.

"After that, Dr. Wright, your role in this will be finished," Ul Quorn said. "You and Captain Lamont will be put aboard a lifeboat and jettisoned...don't worry, we'll program it to make a safe touchdown on Pluto."

"And as for me?" Curt asked.

"You're coming with us, I'm afraid." The seeming warmth of Ul Quorn's smile wasn't reciprocated by the coldness of his eyes. "You're my insurance that nothing aboard your ship is booby-trapped...for if it is, it'll cost you your life as well as mine. And I don't think you're ready to die, are you?"

Curt didn't reply. He knew one thing Ul Quorn didn't: help was on the way. Kuiperians didn't have Anni implants as other *Homo cosmos* transhumans did, so Curt had been unable to communicate with Pluto natives after he and Ezra were captured. Nonetheless, he'd agreed with Livereating Lil that, if neither he nor Ezra got in touch with her within an hour, she was to transmit a priority message to the IPF outpost on Titan Station, telling them that Captain Future and the Futuremen were in trouble and needed help immediately. This would cause a Solar Coalition Navy task force to launch from Phobos Base

At near-light speed, the Navy ships with their SolCol Marine landing teams would make the trip from Mars to Pluto within ten hours. Yet even under the best of circumstances, it would take more than twenty hours for this chain of events to play out. And Ul Quorn wasn't wasting time. The way things were going, the *Liberator* would be gone from the solar system long before the task force reached Pluto.

Curt hated to admit defeat, but it appeared that the Magician of Mars had him boxed in. Nor did he take any pleasure in the knowledge that the man responsible for the murder of his parents was finally dead. If Curt had wanted Victor Corvo to die, he would've killed the man himself. And if Ul Quorn thought having Garson shoot Corvo somehow earned Curt's gratitude, he didn't know Captain Future as well as he might think.

But Curt said nothing. Instead, he kept his thoughts to himself, and waited for a break.

A little more than three hours later, the *Comet* reached its warp ring in parking orbit above Pluto. With Ul Quorn watching his every move from the co-pilot's seat – it was strange not to have Otho or Joan there, but they were still in their cell in Cold Hell – Curt deactivated the drive unit's fantome field.

"Beautiful!" Ul Quorn exclaimed as the torus materialized a few hundred feet off the *Comet's* bow. "An amazing invention, Dr. Wright," he added, peering over his shoulder at the Brain, who was positioned in his niche in the cockpit's aft bulkhead. One of the jovian guards sat behind Curt, and the other kept an eye on Simon. "My compliments. Sometime we ought to discuss how you achieved this."

"Yes, perhaps we shall," Simon said. "I'll look forward to that when I come pay you a visit in Cold Hell."

Ul Quorn said nothing as he turned away from Simon, but the look on his face was priceless. It took a lot for Curt to keep from laughing as he carefully piloted his ship the rest of the way to its rendezvous with the warp torus. The aresian crime lord sat beside him, holding Oog in his lap. Just before the *Comet* lifted off from Pluto, Grag was reactivated and, under heavy guard, marched off the ship at gunpoint and taken to Cold Hell to join the others. The robot had been allowed to take his Eek with him, using the pressurized and heated pet carrier he kept aboard the *Comet* for that purpose, but Ul Quorn wouldn't let him take Oog as well.

"Tell Otho that I'm reclaiming my pet," Ul Quorn had said. "I think it deserves to return to its homeworld after so long…don't you, my friend?" He stroked the wormlike creature as if it was a cat. If the Denebian mimic was happy to know this, it gave no sign, yet Curt noticed that it kept trying to squirm out of Ul Quorn's hands, as if reluctant to be held by the very person who'd found it.

Once the *Comet* was whole again, Curt gave Ul Quorn access to the ship's nav system. Ul Quorn entered the orbital coordinates for the *Liberator,* then Curt took control again and headed for the second rendezvous.

As the *Comet* closed in on the liner, the reasons for its transformation became clear. The big, two-section cradle that had been assembled from the disassembled pieces of the dome section now held the Slingshot. Workmen in vacuum suits floated about the wormhole generator, which had just arrived aboard the orbital freighter parked nearby, one of the prison's service vessels. The aft section was vacant, its sickle-shaped load arms open and waiting. The *Comet* was to dock there, behind the generator, where the warp torus could be hooked up to the generator. It was now obvious why Ul Quorn had chosen the *Titan King*. It took a vessel the size of a space liner to carry both the Slingshot and the *Comet*. Almost of their own volition, Curt's hands wrapped themselves tightly around the control yoke. All he had to do to end this was shove the yoke forward, then slam the throttles forward as well. The *Comet* would be hurled straight into the *Liberator*; his ship would be immediately destroyed, followed seconds later by the subsequent explosion of the liner's fusion engines.

Suicide, yes, but Ul Quorn and Starry Messenger would die, too. And at least he would no longer have to face the fact that he'd fallen into Ul Quorn's snare. A well-conceived snare, yes, but damn it, he'd should've known better. And whatever Ul Quorn and Starry Messenger were plotting, it couldn't be good. So using the *Comet* itself to stop them...well, if this was to be Captain Future's last hurrah, at least he'd make amends.

He took a deep breath ...

–Don't do it, Curtis. Simon's voice, carried to him via Anni. *–If you're considering what I suspect you are, then it's not worth it. There's another way.*

–Really? Curt asked in the same silent way only the two of them could hear. *–And what might that be?*

–I don't know, son, but I'm confident you'll figure it out.

Curt thought about it for a moment, then let his hands relax. *–You're right, Brain. There has to be another way.*

XXIII

The *Liberator's* bridge had changed little from when the ship was called the *Titan King*. The most obvious difference was that someone had painted Starry Messenger's symbol – a circle sprouting a pair of horns, the astrological sign for Mercury – in red across the bulkhead below the forward view screen.

Along the way to the bridge from the service airlock through which Ul Quorn and his guards had brought him and Captain Lamont aboard, Curt had seen plenty of evidence that the *Titan King* had been treated with less than royal respect. Empty bolt-holes and scarred carpets showed where unnecessary furniture and decorative fixtures had been removed; discarded food containers and other items of trash floated in the corridors, and in the crew's mess, someone had amused themselves by throwing steak knives from the kitchen at a portrait of President Carthew they'd printed out and taped to the wall.

Curt didn't have to ask Henri Lamont whether any of this offended him. One look at the liner's former captain told him that Lamont regarded it all as nothing less than blasphemy. Lamont now stood at the back of the command center, seething with silent fury as he observed the final preparations for the launch to hyperspace. Curt couldn't help but feel a certain pity for the man. Two of his former bridge officers – Harl al-Sarakka, the jovian helmsman, and Kars Kaastro, the aresian communications officer – had committed mutiny by joining Ul Quorn's gang when they'd hijacked the liner. They were now seated at their respective stations, doing their best to ignore their former skipper.

Lamont wasn't the only person on the bridge to find himself in the company of someone who'd betrayed him. Only a few minutes later, the bridge door slid open and who should come in but Ashi Lanyr. She was accompanied by N'Rala, the statuesque aresian woman who was Ul Quorn's paramour. As the two women used the ceiling handrails to pull themselves into the control room, Ashi's eyes met Curt's. For a long instant, the two regarded one another, neither willing to speak, but not willing to be the first to look away. Then, Ashi hastily turned her head and didn't look at him as N'Rala led her to a pair of empty chairs in the back of the control room.

As for Lamont, once he'd been brought to the bridge and entered the appropriate passwords that turned final command of the massive ship over to Ul Quorn, the only reason he was still there was to assure Curt and Simon's cooperation. Curt knew, without being told, that if he or the Brain resisted in any way, Ul Quorn – who was seated in the command chair, Lamont's former station – wouldn't think twice about ordering the terran standing beside Lamont to shoot him. Indeed, the only way any of them would live through the next few minutes was if Curt, Simon and Tiko Thrinn obeyed Ul Quorn's orders.

The three of them were now grouped around the engineering station, entering the final instructions to the main AI that would interface the dark energy generator of *Comet's* warp drive with the Slingshot and place both under the control of the *Liberator's* bridge. As he watched, the Brain reached forward with one of his manipulators to type in the command that would activate the generator.

"Ready, Thrinn?" Simon asked. The aresian physicist nodded, albeit reluctantly. "All right, then…" The Brain's eyestalks moved toward Curt. "Start the countdown, lad."

"Stand by to commence countdown, five seconds to mark." Without looking away from the console, Curt raised his voice so that it could be heard throughout the bridge. "Five… four… three… two… one… mark!"

He reached forward and stabbed *Enter* on the main keyboard. There was no indication that anything was different, yet the screen displays at all the major bridge stations suddenly changed, with a five-minute countdown starting at the top of each screen."

All right," Curt said, straightening up to look at Ul Quorn. "All systems are now under AI control for wormhole formation and insertion. We've got t-minus –" he glanced at the nearest screen "– four minutes and forty-seven seconds."

"Very good. I'm impressed." The Magician of Mars sat cross-legged in the command chair, calmly stroking Oog in his lap. "And there's nothing more that needs to be done?"

"No." Tiko Thrinn turned about in his chair. "From here on, the AIs are in command. I've entered the galactic coordinates for the Deneb system, and a return flight to our home system has been entered as well."

"All you need to do to get home is tell the AI you're ready to return." Simon's eyestalks twisted about to regard Ul Quorn. "Everything is preprogrammed. You'll only need Mr. al-Sarakka to act as pilot during planetary rendezvous maneuvers." As usual, the jovian helmsman offered only a sullen grunt as his response.

"Very well then." A smile appeared upon Ul Quorn's face that was somehow both ingratiating and taunting. "Dr. Tiko, Dr. Wright...the two of you have fulfilled your end of the agreement, so I'll fulfill mine." He turned to a hard-faced young terran woman standing beside him. "Would you be so kind as to escort them down to the lifeboat deck?" He looked at the two scientists again. "Lifeboat Six has been reserved for your use. It's already been programmed to carry you safely to the ground...you'll land in the Sputnik Planum about three kilometers southeast of Bernard's Landing."

Without a word, Tiko Thrinn stood up and headed for the door. Simon didn't follow him, though. Instead, his eyestalks turned toward Curt. "I'm not leaving without you," he said.

"Yes, you are." Curt pointed to the door, where Tiko and Ul Quorn's henchwoman stood waiting. "There's nothing you can do for me. Go on, get out of here...please."

Simon hesitated another moment. "All right, then," he said at last, "so be it. Good luck, lad." The Brain was still wearing his EVA body; its reaction-control thrusters swiveled and emitted a whisper-soft burst, and he floated toward the door. Curt watched as the Brain and Tiko Thrinn left the bridge, then he looked at Ul Quorn again. "What about him?" he asked, cocking a thumb at Lamont. "Aren't going to let him go, too?"

"No." Ul Quorn shook his head. "I've changed my mind about Captain Lamont. He's going to stay with us, as our guest."

"Why?"

"Because I'll still need a hostage to keep you in line." Ul Quorn spoke of Lamont as if the captain wasn't standing behind him, glaring. "I don't think I can trust you, M'sieur Newton, so he's going to remain with us."

Lamont still wasn't speaking, yet the look on his face told Curt that he was on the verge of losing his temper and physically assaulting Ul Quorn. Curt was all for it, but he knew that both of them would be cut down by Ul Quorn's bodyguards before they even got close. If only they had something to distract them...

A faint beep from the helm. Harl al-Sarakka checked the readout on his screen. "Lifeboat Six jettisoned," he reported. "Artificial gravity online in thirty seconds and counting."

A half-minute later a klaxon sounded, warning everyone that the warp bubble forming around the *Liberator* was creating a localized 1-g gravity field. Curt felt weight return to him and he was ready for it, relaxing his body and letting his legs absorb the mass.

"Well...that's better." Like everyone else seated in the bridge, Ul Quorn unfastened the lap strap that had been holding him in his chair. He glanced at the alien mimic in his lap and scowled. "Y'know," he said to no one particular, "I used to be able to get it to change into a white Persian cat, but it seems to not want to do that for me any longer." He looked up at Curt. "What have you done with it? It doesn't seem to like me anymore."

"Maybe Oog has better taste in people now." As Curt said this, an idea occurred to him.

In the years since Otho adopted Oog, he and Curt had made a pastime of teaching it new tricks. One of them was to respond to telepathic commands sent by someone who wasn't actually touching it. Oog no longer had to have someone physically holding onto it; an imaginary projection of a creature approximately its own size, pictured in the mind of someone standing nearby, was sufficient.

Curt remembered a rare Earth animal he'd once seen in a conservatory in Chicago, an inhabitant of the North American continent that had been saved from extinction during the climate crisis of the twenty-first century by cloning genetic material stored in a gene bank. Fastening his gaze on Oog, Curt concentrated on a mind's eye image of this peculiar animal.

Oog telepathically caught the image and changed its form accordingly.

An instant later, Ul Quorn's hand came to rest on the needle-sharp quills of the porcupine that had just materialized in his lap.

He screamed an obscenity and leaped up to hurl Oog away; the moment he was out of the command chair, Curt threw himself at Ul Quorn.

"Lamont, stop the countdown!" he yelled.

Henri Lamont reacted at once. As Curt sailed into Ul Quorn and tackled him, Lamont dove for the command chair. The small control pad embedded within the right armrest included the keypad he'd need to enter the passcode that would enable him to scrub the launch. If Curt could just buy him a few precious seconds…

"Bastard!" Ul Quorn snarled. He'd somehow managed to stay on his feet; he shoved Curt away and threw a punch at him at the same time. "I knew you couldn't be trusted!"

Curt didn't waste time or breath on repartee. Ul Quorn's fist connected with the side of his face, but not hard enough to stop or stun him. Curt let his neck relax and his head roll with the punch, and responded with one of his own. Ul Quorn was tougher than he looked, though; his right arm shot up to deflect Curt's fist, then his left leg came up in a savage kick that caught Curt in the stomach.

Caught by surprise, Curt grunted and doubled over. As he struggled to stand up straight, he caught a glimpse of Ashi. She'd left her seat and looked as if she was about to…what? Throw herself into the fight? On whose side?

No time for her. Curt looked around at Lamont, saw that he was having problems of his own. The captain had made it to the command chair, but no sooner had he begun to enter the passcode that would halt the countdown – Curt caught a glimpse of the chronometer: -00.00.56, less than a minute remaining – than al-Sarakka was on him. Lamont did his best to fight off the helmsman, but the giant jovian was like an angry bear, another near-extinct Earth animal.

Then Ul Quorn came at him again, this time with an open-hand karate chop. Curt dodged the blow; he used his momentum to spin about, bring up his right leg, and slam the sole of his boot into Ul Quorn's side. The Magician of Mars grunted and fell forward, but recovered in time to intercept Curt as he dove for the command chair.

As Ul Quorn tackled him, Curt heard a dull snap from close beside him, the place near the command chair where Lamont and al-Sarakka had been just a moment ago. He looked around in time to see Lamont dangling within the jovian's arms, the helmsman's massive hands wrapped around his former commander's head and throat. In a moment of cold horror, Curt realized what had just happened: Harl al-Sakarra had just broken Henri Lamont's neck.

At that instant, the klaxon bellowed again, and suddenly it felt as if the entire ship was an elevator whose cables had been severed. Curt lost his footing; he fell forward, and as he did, there was a sensation of being stretched, like his body had become soft taffy that some god-child was pulling apart.

Curt gasped as darkness, black and starless, closed around him. And in that instant, in a place where time and space lost meaning, the *Liberator* plunged through the wormhole it created, taking with it Captain Future and everyone else.

The Harpers of Titan

I

SHADOWED MOON

*H*is name was Simon Wright, and once he had been a man like other men. Now he was a man no longer, but a living brain, housed in a metal case, nourished by serum instead of blood, provided with artificial senses and means of motion.

The body of Simon Wright, that had known the pleasures and the ills of physical existence, had long ago mingled with dust. But the mind of Simon Wright lived on, brilliant and unimpaired.

The ridge lifted, gaunt and rocky, along the rim of the lichen forest, the giant growths crowding to the very crest and down the farther slope into the valley.

Here and there was a clearing around what might once have been a temple, now long fallen into ruin. The vast ragged shapes of the lichens loomed above it, wrinkled and wind-torn and sad. Now and again, a little breeze came and set them to rustling with a sound like muted weeping, shaking down a rotten, powdery dust.

Simon Wright was weary of the ridge and the dun-gray forest, weary of waiting. Three of Titan's nights had passed since he and Grag and Otho and Curt Newton, whom the System knew better as Captain Future, had hidden their ship down in the lichen-forest and had waited here on the ridge for a man who did not come.

This was the fourth night of waiting, under the incredible glory of Titan's sky. But even the pageant of Saturn, girdled with blazing Rings and attended by the brilliant swarm of moons, failed to lift Simon's mental spritis. Somehow, the beauty above only accentuated the dreariness below.

Curt Newton said sharply, "If Keogh doesn't come tonight, I'm going down there and look for him."

He looked outward through a rift of lichens, to the valley where Moneb lay – a city indistinct with night and distance, picked out here and there with the light of torches.

Simon spoke, his voice coming precise and metallic through the artificial resonator.

"Keogh's message warned us on no account to go into the city. Be patient, Curtis. He will come."

Otho nodded. Otho, the lean, lithe android who was so exactly human that only a disturbing strangeness in his pointed face and green, bright eyes betrayed him.

"Apparently," Otho said, "there's a devil of a mess going on in Moneb, and we're liable to make it worse if we go tramping in before we know what it's all about."

The manlike metal form of Grag moved impatiently in the shadows with a dull clanking sound, His booming voice crashed loud against the stillness.

"I'm like Curt," he said. I'm tired of waiting."

"We are all tired," said Simon. "But we must wait. From Keogh's message, I judge that he is neither a coward nor a fool. He knows the situation. We do not. We must not endanger him by impatience."

Curt sighed. "I know it." He settled back on the block of stone where he was sitting. "I only hope he makes it soon. These infernal lichens are getting on my nerves."

Poised, effortlessly upon the unseen magnetic beams that were his limbs, Simon watched and brooded. Only in a detached way could he appreciate the picture he presented to others – a small square metal case, with a strange face of artificial lens-eyes and resonator-mouth, hovering in the darkness.

To himself, Simon seemed almost a bodiless ego. He could not see his own strange body. He was conscious only of the steady, rhythmic throbbing of the serum-pump that served as his heart, and of the visual and auditory sensations that his artificial sense-organs gathered for him.

His lenslike eyes were capable of better vision under all conditions than the human eye, but even so, he could not penetrate the shifting, tumultuous shadows of the valley. It remained a mystery of shaking moonlight, mist and darkness.

It looked peaceful. And yet, the message of this stranger, Keogh, had cried for help against an evil too great for him to fight alone.

Simon was acutely conscious of the dreary rustling of the lichens. His microphonic auditory system could hear and distinguish each separate tiny note too faint for normal ears, so that the rustling became a weaving, shifting pattern of sound, as of ghostly voices whispering – a sort of symphony of despair.

Pure fancy, and Simon Wright was not given to fancies. Yet in these nights of waiting, he had developed a definite sense of foreboding. He reasoned now that this sad whispering of the forest was responsible, his brain reacting to the repeated stimulus of a sound-pattern.

Like Curt, he hoped Keogh would come soon.

Time passed. The Rings filled the sky with supernal fire, and the moons went splendidly on their eternal way, bathed in the milky glow of Saturn. The lichens would not cease from their dusty weeping. Now and again, Curt Newton rose and went restlessly back and forth across the clearing. Otho watched him, sitting still, his slim body bent like a steel bow. Grag remained where he was, a dark immobile giant in the shadows, dwarfing even Newton's height.

Then, abruptly, there was a sound different from all other sounds. Simon heard, and listened, and after a moment, he said:

"There are two men, climbing the slope from the valley, coming this way."

Otho sprang up. Curt voiced a short, sharp, "Ah!" and said, "Better take cover, until we're sure."

The four melted into the darkness.

Simon was so close to the strangers that he might have reached out one of his force-beams and touched them. They came into the clearing, breathing heavily from the long climb, looking eagerly about. One was a tall man, very tall, with a gaunt width of shoulder and a fine head. The other was shorter, broader, moving with a bearlike gait. Both were Earthmen, with the unmistakable stamp of the frontiers on them, and the hardness of physical labor. Both men were armed.

They stopped. The hope went out of them, and the tall man said despairingly, "They failed us. They didn't come. Dan, they didn't come!"

Almost, the tall man wept.

"I guess your message didn't get through," the other man said. His voice, too, was leaden. "I don't know, Keogh. I don't know what we'll do now. I guess we might as well go back."

Curt Newton spoke out of the darkness. "Hold on a minute. It's all right."

Curt moved out into the open space, his lean face and red hair clear in the moonlight. "It's he," said the stocky man. "It's Captain Future." His voice was shaken with relief.

Keogh smiled, a smile without much humor in it. "You thought I might be dead and someone else might keep the appointment. Not a far-fetched assumption. I've been so closely watched that I dared not try to get away before. I only just managed it tonight."

He broke off, staring, as Grag came striding up, shaking the ground with his tread. Otho moved in from beyond him, light as a leaf. Simon joined them, gliding from among the shadows.

Keogh laughed, a little shakily. "I'm glad to see you. If you only knew how glad I am to see you all!"

"And me," said the stocky man. He added, "I'm Harker."

"My friend," Keogh told the Futuremen. "For many years, my friend." Then, he hesitated, looking earnestly at Curt. "You will help me? I've held back down there in Moneb so far. I've kept the people quiet. I've tried to give them courage when they need it, but I'm only one man. That;s a frail peg on which to hang the fate of a city."

Curt nodded gravely. "We'll do what we can. Otho – Grag! Keep watch, just in case."

Grag and Otho disappeared again. Curt looked expectantly at Keogh and Harker. The breeze had steadied to a wind, and Simon was conscious that it was rising, bringing a deeper plaint from the lichens.

Keogh sat down on a block of stone and began to talk. Hovering near him, Simon listened, watching Keogh's face. It was a good face. A wise man, Simon thought, and a strong one, exhausted now by effort and long fear.

"I was the first Earthman to come into the valley, years ago," Keogh said. "I liked the men of Moneb and they liked me. When the miners began to come in, I saw to it that there was no trouble between them and the natives. I married a girl of Moneb, daughter of one of the chief men. She's dead now, but I have a son here. And I'm one of the councilors, the only man of foreign blood ever allowed in the Inner City.

"So you see, I've swung a lot of weight and have used it to keep peace here between native and outlander. But **now!**"

He shook his head. "There have always been men in Moneb who hated to see Earthmen and Earth civilization come in and lessen their own influence. They've hated the Eartmen who live in New Town and work the mines. They'd have tried long ago to force them out, and would have embroiled Moneb in a hopeless struggle, if they'd dared defy tradition and use their one possible weapon. Now, they're bolder and are planning to use that weapon."

Curt Newton looked at him keenly. "What is this weapon, Keogh?"

Keogh's answer was a question. "You Futuremen know these worlds well – I suppose you've heard of the Harpers?"

Simon Wright felt a shock of surprise. He saw incredulous amazement on Curt Newton's face.

"You don't mean that your malcontents plan to use the **Harpers** as a weapon?"

Keogh nodded somberly. "They do."

Memories of old days on Titan were flashing through Simon's mind; the strange form of life that dwelt deep in the great forests, the unforgettable beauty wedded to dreadful danger.

"The Harpers could be a weapon, yes," he said, after a moment. "But the weapon would slay those who wielded it, unless they were protected from it."

"Long ago," Keogh answered, "the men of Moneb had such a protection. They used the Harpers, then. But use of them was so disastrous that it was forbidden, put under a tabu."

"Now, those who wish to force out the Earthmen here plan to break that tabu. They want to bring in the Harpers, and use them."

Harker added, "Things were all right until the old king died. He was a man. His son is a weakling. The fanatics against outland civilization have got to him, and he's afraid of his own shadow. Keogh has been holding him on his feet, against them."

Simon saw the almost worshipful trust in Harker's eyes as he glanced at his friend. "They've tried to kill Keogh, of course," Harker said. "With him gone, there's be no leader against them." – Keogh's voice rose, to be heard over the booming and thrumming of the lichens.

"A full council has been called for two days from now. That will be the time of decision – whether we, or the breakers of the tabu, will rule in Moneb. And I know, as I know truth, that some kind of trap as been set for me.

"That's where I will need you Futuremen's help, most desperately. But you must not be seen in the town. Any strangers now would excite suspicion, and you are too well known, and –" he glanced at Simon and added apologetically, "distinctive."

He paused. In that pause, the boom and thunder of the lichen was like the slatting of great sails in the wind, and Simon could not hear the little furtive sound from behind him until it was too late – a second too late.

A man leaped into the clearing. Simon had a fleeting glimpse of copper-gold limbs and a killer's face, and a curious weapon raised. Simon spoke, but the bright small dart was already fled.

In the same breath, Curt turned and drew and fired.

The man dropped. Out of the shadows another gun flashed, and they heard Otho's fierce cry.

There was a timeless instant when no one moved, and then Otho came back into the clearing. "There were only two of them, I think."

"They followed us!" Harker exclaimed. "They followed us up here to –"

He had been turning, as he spoke. He suddenly stopped speaking, and then cried out Keogh's name.

Keogh lay face down in the powdery dust. From out his temple stood a slim bronzed shaft little larger than a needle, and where it pierced the flesh was one dark drop of blood.

Simon hovered over the Earthman. His sensitive beams touched the throat, the breast, lifted one lax eyelid.

Simon said, without hope, "He still lives."

II

UNEARTHLY STRATAGEM

G rag carried Keogh through the forest and, tall man that Keogh was, he seemed like a child in the robot's mighty arms. The wind howled, and the lichens shook and thundered, and it was growing darker.

"Hurry!" said Harker. "Hurry – there may still be a chance!"

His face had the white, staring look that comes with shock. Simon was still possessed of emotion – sharper, clearer emotions than before, he thought divorced as they were from the chemical confusions of the flesh. Now he knew a great pity for Harker.

"The *Comet* is just ahead," Curt told him.

Presently they saw the ship, a shadowed bulk of metal lost among the giant growths. Swiftly they took Keogh in, and Grag laid him carefully on the table in the tiny laboratory. He was still breathing, but Simon knew that it would not be for very long.

The laboratory of the *Comet*, for all its cramped size, was fitted with medical equipment comparable to most hospitals – most of it designed for its particular purpose by Simon himself, and by Curt Newton. It had been used many times before for the saving of lives. Now the two of them, Simon and Curt together, worked feverishly to save Keogh.

Curt wheeled a marvellously compact adaptation of the Fraser unit into place. Within seconds, the tubes were clamped into Keogh's arteries and the pumps were working, keeping the blood flowing normally, feeding in a stimulant solution directly to the heart. The oxygen unit was functioning. Presently Curt nodded.

"Pulse and respiration normal. Now let's have a look at the brain."

He swung the ultrafluoroscope into position and switched it on. Simon looked into the screen, hovering close to Curt's shoulder.

"The frontal lobe is torn beyond repair," he said. "See the tiny barbs on that dart? Deterioration of the cells has already set in."

Harker spoke from the doorway. "Can't you do something? Can't you save him?" He stared into Curt's face for a moment, and then his head dropped forward and he said dully, "No, of course you can't. I knew it when he was hit."

All the strength seemed to drain out of him. He leaned against the door, a man tired and beaten and sad beyond endurance.

"It's bad enough to lose a friend. But now everything he fought for is lost, too. The fanatics will win, and they'll turn loose something that will destroy not only the Earthmen here, but the entire population of Moneb too, in the long run."

Tears began to run slowly from Harker's eyes. He did not seem to notice them. He said, to no one, to the universe, "Why couldn't I have seen him in time? Why couldn't I have killed him – in time?"

For a long, long moment, Simon looked at Harker. Then he glanced again into the screen, and then aside at Curt, who nodded and slowly switched it off. Curt began to remove the tubes of the Fraser unit from Keogh's wrists.

Simon said, "Wait, Curtis. Leave them as they are."

Curt straightened, a certain startled wonder in his eyes. Simon glided to where Harker stood, whiter and more stricken than the dead man on the table.

Simon spoke his name three times, before he roused himself to answer.

"Yes?"

"How much courage have you, Harker? As much as Keogh? As much as I?"

Harker shook his head.

"There are times when courage doesn't help a bit."

"Listen to me, Harker! Have you the courage to walk beside Keogh into Moneb, knowing that he is dead?"

The eyes of the stocky man widened. And Curt Newton came to Simon and said in a strange voice, "What are you thinking of?"

"I am thinking of a brave man who died in the act of seeking help from us. I am thinking of many innocent men and women who will die unless...Harker, it is true, is it not, that the success of your fight depended on Keogh?"

Harker's gaze dwelt upon the body stretched on the table – a body that breathed and pulsed with the semblance of life borrowed from the sighing pumps.

"That is true," he said. "That's why they killed him. He was the leader. With him gone –" Harker's broad hands made a gesture of utter loss.

"Then it must not be known that Keogh died."

Curt said harshly, "No! Simon, you can't do it!"

"Why not, Curtis? You are perfectly capable of completing the operation."

"They've killed the man once. They'll be ready to do it again. Simon, you can't risk yourself! Even if I could do the operation – no!"

Something queerly pleading came into Curt's gray eyes. "This is my kind of job, Simon. Mine and Grag's and Otho's. Let us do it."

"And how will you do it?" Simon asked. "By force? By reasoning? You are not omnipotent, Curtis. Nor are Grag and Otho. You, all three of you, would be going into certain death. And even more certain defeat. And I know you. You **would** go."

Simon paused. It seemed to him suddenly that he had gone mad to contemplate what he was about to do. And yet, it was the only way – the only possible chance of preventing an irretrievable disaster.

Simon knew what the Harpers could do, in the wrong hands. He knew what would happen to the Earthmen in New Town. And he knew too what retribution for that would overtake the many guiltless people of Moneb, as well as the few guilty ones.

He glanced beyond Harker and saw Grag standing there, and Otho beside him, his green eyes very bright, and Simon thought, I made them both, I and Roger Newton. I gave them hearts and minds and courage. Some day they will perish, but it will not be because I failed them.

And there was Curt, stubborn, reckless, driven by the demon of his own loneliness, a bitter searcher after knowledge, a stranger to his own kind.

Simon thought, *We made him so, Otho and Grag and I. And we wrought him too well. There is too much iron in him. He will break, but never bend – and I will not have him broken because of me!*

Harker said, very slowly, "I understand."

Simon explained, "Keogh's body is whole. Only the brain was destroyed. If the body were supplied with another brain – mine – Keogh would seem to live again, to finish his task in Moneb."

Harker stood for a long monent without speaking. Then he whispered, "Is that possible?"

"Quite possible. Not easy, not even safe – but possible."

Harker's hands clenched into fists. Something, a light that might have been hope, crept back into his eyes.

"Only we five," said Simon, "know that Keogh died. There would be no difficulty there. And I know the language of Titan, as I know most of the System tongues.

"But I would still need help – a guide, who knew Keogh's life and could enable me to live it for the short time that is necessary. You, Harker. And I warn you, it will not be easy."

Harker's voice was low, but steady. "If you can do the one thing, I can do the other."

Curt Newton said angrily, "No one is going to do anything of the sort. Simon, I won't have any part of it!"

The stormy look that Simon knew so well had come into Curt's face. If Simon had been able to, he would have smiled. Instead, he spoke exactly as he had spoken so many times before, long ago when Curt Newton was a small red-headed boy playing in the lonely corridors of the laboratory hidden under Tycho, with no companions but the robot, the android, and Simon, himself.

"You will do as I say, Curtis!" He turned to the others. "Grag, take Mr. Harker into the main cabin. See that he sleeps, for he will need his strength. Otho, Curtis will want your help."

Otho came in and shut the door. He glanced from Simon to Curt and back again, his eyes brilliant with a certain acid amusement. Curt stood where he was, his jaw set, unmoving.

Simon glided over to the cabinets built solidly against one wall. Using the wonderfully adaptable force-beams more skillfully than a man uses his hands, he took from them the needful things – the trephine saw, the clamps and sutures, the many-shaped delicate knives. And the other things, that had set modern surgery so far ahead of the crude Twentieth Century techniques. The compounds that prevented bleeding, the organic chemicals that promoted cell regeneration so rapidly and fully that a wound would heal within hours and leave no scar, the stimulants and anaesthetics that prevented shock, the neurone compounds.

The UV tube was pulsing overhead, sterilizing everything in the laboratory. Simon, whose vision was better and touch more sure than that of any surgeon dependent on human form, made the preliminary incision in Keogh's skull.

Curt Newton had still not moved. His face was as set and stubborn as before, but there was a pallor about it now, something of desperation.

Simon said sharply, "Curtis!"

"Pay particular attention, Curtis, to the trigeminal, glossopharyngeal, facial –"

"I know all about that," said Curt, with a peculiar irritation.

"– pneumogastric, spinal accessory, and hypoglossal nerves," Simon finished. Vials and syringes were laid in a neat row. "Here is the anaesthetic to be introduced into my serum-stream. And immediately after the operation, this is to be injected beneath the dura and pia mater."

Curt nodded. His hands had stopped shaking, working now with swift, sure skill. His mouth had thinned to a grim line.

Simon thought, *He'll do. He'll always do.*

There was a moment, then, of waiting. Simon looked down at the man John Keogh and of a sudden fear took hold of him, a deep terror of what he was about to do.

He was content as he was. Once, many years before, he had made his choice between extinction and his present existence. The genius of Curt's own father had saved him then, given him new life, and Simon had made peace with that life, strange as it was, and turned it to good use. He had discovered the advantages of his new form – the increased skills, the ability to think clearly with a mind unfettered by useless and uncontrollable impulses of the flesh. He had learned to be grateful for them.

And now, after all these years…

He thought, *I cannot do it, after all! I, too, am afraid – not of dying, but of life.*

And yet, beneath that fear was longing, a hunger that Simon had thought mercifully dead these many years.

The longing to be once again a man, a human being clothed in flesh.

The cold, clear mind of Simon Wright, the precise, logical, unwavering mind, reeled under the impact of these mingled dreads and hungers. They leaped up full stature from their graves in his subconscious. He was shocked that he could still be prey to emotion, and the voice of his mind cried out, *I cannot do it! No, I cannot!*

Curt said quietly, "All ready, Simon."

Slowly, very slowly, Simon moved and came to rest beside John Keogh. He saw Otho watching him, with a look of pain and understanding, and – yes, envy. Being unhuman himself, Otho would know, where others could only guess.

Curt's face was cut from stone. The serum-pump broke its steady rhythm, and then went on.

Simon Wright passed quietly into the darkness.

III

ONCE BORN OF FLESH

Hearing came first. A distant confusion of sounds, seeming very dull and blurred. Simon's first thought was that something had gone wrong with his auditory mechanism. Then a chill wing of memory brushed him, and in its wake came a pang of fear, and a sense of **wrongness**.

It was dark. Why should it be so dark in the *Comet*? From far off, someone called his name. "Simon! Simon, open your eyes!"

Eyes?

Again that dull inchoate terror. His mind was heavy. It refused to function, and the throb of the serum-pump was gone.

The serum-pump, Simon thought. *It has stopped, and I am dying!*

He must call for help. That had happened once before, and Curt had saved him. He cried out, "Curtis, the serum-pump has stopped!"

The voice was not his own, and it was formed so strangely.

"I'm here, Simon. Open your eyes." A long unused series of motor relays clicked over in Simon's brain at that repeated command. Without conscious volition he raised his eyelids. Someone's eyelids, surely not his own! He had not had eyelids for many years!

He saw.

Vision like the hearing, dim and blurred. The familiar laboratory seemed to swim in a wavering haze. Curt's face, and Otho's, and above them the looming form of Grag and a strange man... No, not strange; he had a name and Simon knew it – Harker.

That name started the chain, and Simon remembered. Memory pounced upon him, worried him, tore him, and now he could **feel the fear** – the physical anguish of it, the sweating, the pounding of the heart, the painful contraction of the great bodily ganglia.

"Raise your hand, Simon. Raise your right hand." There was a strained undertone in Curt's voice. Simon understood. Curt was afraid he might not have done things properly.

Uncertainly, like a child who has not yet learned coordination, Simon raised his right hand. Then his left. He looked at them for an endless moment and let them fall. Drops of saline moisture stung his eyes, and he remembered them. He remembered tears.

"You're all right," Curt said shakily. He helped Simon raise his head and held a glass to his lips." Can you drink this? It will clear away the fog, give you strength."

Simon drank, and the act of drinking had wonder in it.

The potion counteracted the remaining effects of the anaesthetic. Sight and hearing cleared, and he had his mind under control again. He lay still for some time, trying to adjust himself to the all but forgotten sensations of the flesh.

The little things. The crispness of a sheet against the skin, the warmth, the pleasure of relaxed lips. The memory of sleep.

He sighed, and in that, too, there was wonder. "Give me your hand, Curtis. I will stand."

Curt was on one side, Otho on the other, steadying him. And Simon Wright, in the body of John Keogh, rose from the table where he had lain and stood upright, a man and whole.

By the doorway, Harker fell forward in a dead faint.

Simon looked at him, the strong stocky man crumpled on the floor, his face gray and sick. He said, with a queer touch of pity for all humanity, "I told him it would not be easy."

But even Simon had not realized just how hard it would be.

There were so many things to be learned all over again. Long used to a weightless, effortless ease of movement, this tall rangy body he now inhabited seemed heavy and awkward, painfully slow. He had great difficulty in managing it. At first, his attempts to walk were a series of ungainly staggerings wherein he must cling to something to keep from falling.

His sense of balance had to undergo a complete readjustment. And the dullness of his sight and hearing bothered him. That was only comparative, he knew – Keogh's sight and hearing had been excellent, by all human standards. But they lacked the precision, the selectivity, the clarity to which Simon had become accustomed. He felt as though his senses were somehow muffled, as by a veil.

And it was a strange thing, when he stumbled or made an incautious movement, to feel pain again.

But as he began to gain control over this complicated bulk of bone and muscle and nerve, Simon found himself taking joy in it. The endless variety of sensory and tactile impressions, the feeling of life, of warm blood flowing, the knowing of heat and cold and hunger were fascinating.

Once born of flesh, he thought, and clenched his hands together. *What have I done? What madness have I done?*

He must not think of that, nor of himself. He must think of nothing but the task to be done, in the name of John Keogh who was dead.

Harker recovered from his faint. "I'm sorry," he muttered. "It was just that I saw him – you – rise up and stand, it –" He did not finish. "I'm all right, now. You don't have to worry."

Simon noticed that he kept his eyes averted as much as possible. But there was a dogged look about him that said he told the truth.

"We ought to get back as soon as you can make it," Harker said. "We – Keogh and I, have been gone too long as it is."

He added, "There's just one thing. What about Dion?"

"Dion?"

"Keogh's son."

Simon said slowly, "No need to tell the boy. He could not understand, and it will only torture him."

Mercifully, he thought, *the time will be short.* But he wished that Keogh had not had a son.

Curt interrupted. "Simon, I've been talking to Harker. The council is tonight, only a few hours away. And you will have to go alone into the Inner City, for there Harker is not allowed to enter.

"But Otho and I are going to try to get around Moneb and into the council hall, secretly. Harker tells me that was Keogh's idea, and it's a good one – if it works, Grag will stay with the ship, on call if necessary."

He handed Simon two objects, a small mono-wave audio disc and a heavy metal box only four inches square.

"We'll keep in touch with the audios," he said. "The other is a hasty adaptation of the *Comet's* own repellor field, but tuned for sonic vibrations. I had to rob two of the coil units. What do you think of it?"

Simon examined the tiny box, the compact, cunning interior arrangement of oscillators, the capsule power unit, the four complicated grids.

"The design might have been further simplified, Curtis – but, under the circumstances, a creditable job. It will serve very well, in case of necessity."

"Let's hope," said Curt feelingly, "that there won't be any such case." He looked at Simon and smiled. His eyes held a deep pride and admiration.

"Good luck," he said.

Simon held out his hand. It was long since he had done that. He was amazed to find his voice unsteady.

"Take care," he said. "All of you."

He turned and went out, going still abut uncertainly, and behind him he heard Curt speaking low and savagely to Harker.

"If you let anything happen to him, I'll kill you with my own hands!"

Simon smiled.

Harker joined him. And they went together through the lichen forest, ghostly under the dim, far Sun. The tall growths were silent now that the wind had died. And as they went, Harker talked of Moneb and the men and women who dwelt there. Simon listened, knowing that his life depended on remembering what he heard.

But even that necessity could not occupy more than one small part of his mind. The rest of it was busy with other things – the bitter smell of dust, the chill bite of the air in the shaded places, the warmth of the sun in the clearings, the intricate play of muscles necessary to the taking of a step, the rasp of lichen fronds over unprotected skin, the miracle of breathing, of sweating, of grasping an object with five fingers of flesh.

The little things one took for granted. The small, miraculous incredible things that one never noticed until they were gone.

He had seen the forest before as a dun-gray monochrome, heard it as a pattern of rustling sound. It had been without temperature, scent or feel. Now it had all of these things. Simon was overwhelmed with a flood of impressions, poignant almost beyond enduring.

He gathered strength and sureness as he went. By the time he breasted the slope of the ridge, he could find pleasure in the difficulty of climbing, scrambling up over treacherous slides of dust, choking, coughing as the acrid powder invaded his lungs.

Harker swore, shambling bearlike up the steep way among the lichens. And suddenly, Simon laughed. He could not have said what made him do so. But it was good to laugh again.

They avoided the clearing by common consent. Harker led the way, lower down across the ridge. They came out onto the open ground, and Simon was touched beyond measure to find that he had a shadow.

They paused to get their breath, and Harker glanced sidelong at Simon, his eyes full of a strange curiousity.

"How does it feel?" he asked. "How does it feel to be a man again?"

Simon did not answer. He could not. There were no words. He looked away from Harker, out over the valley that lay so quiet under the shadowy Sun. He was filled with a strange excitement, so that he felt himself tremble. As though suddenly frightened by what he had said, and all the things that were implicit in that question, Harker turned suddenly and plunged down the slope, almost running, and Simon followed. Once, he slipped and caught himself, gashing his hand against a rock. He stood motionless, watching with wondering eyes the slow red drops that ran from the cut, until Harker had called him three times by Keogh's name, and once by his own.

They avoided the New Town. "No use asking for trouble," Harker said, and led the way past it down a ravine. But they could see it in the distance, a settlement of metalloy houses on a shoulder of the ridge, below the black mouth of the mines. Simon thought the town was strangely quiet.

"See the shutters on the windows?" Harker asked. "See the barricades in the streets? They're waiting, waiting for tonight."

He did not speak again. At the foot of the ridge, they came to an open plain, dotted with clumps of grayish scrub. They began to cross it, toward the outskirts of the city.

But as they approached Moneb, a group of men came running to meet them. At their head, Simon saw a tall, dark-haired boy.

Harker said, "That is your son."

His skin a lighter gold, his face a mixture of Keogh's and something of a softer beauty, his eyes very direct and proud, Dion was what Simon would have expected.

He felt a sense of guilt as greeted the boy by name. Yet mingled with it was a strange feeling of pride. He thought suddenly, *I wish that I had had a son like this, in the old days before I changed.*

And then, desperately, *I must not think these things! The lure of the flesh is pulling me back.*

Dion was breathless with haste, his face showing the marks of sleeplessness and worry.

"Father, we've scoured the valley for you! Where have you been?"

Simon started the explanation that he had concerted with Harker, but the boy cut him short, racing from one thing to another in an urgent flood of words.

"You didn't come, and we were afraid something had happened to you. And while you were gone, they advanced the time of the council! They hoped you wouldn't come back at all, but if you did, they were going to make sure it was too late."

Dion's strong young hands gripped Simon's arm. "They're already gathering in the council hall! Come on. There may still be time, but we must hurry!"

Harker looked grimly over the boy's head at Simon. "It's come already."

With Keogh's impatient son, and the men with him, they hurried on into the city.

Houses of mud brick, generations old, and towering above them the wall of the Inner City, and above that still the roofs and squat, massive towers of the palaces and temples, washed with a kind of lime and painted with ocher and crimson.

The air was full of smells – of food and the smoke of cooking fires, acrid-sweet, of dust, of human bodies oiled and fragrant and musky, of old brick crumbling in the sun, of beasts in pens, of unknown spices. Simon breathed them deeply, and listened to the echo of his footsteps ring hollow from the walls. He felt the rising breeze cold on his face that was damp with sweat. And again, the excitement shook him, and with it came a sort of awe at the magnificence of human sensation.

I had forgotten so much, he thought. *And how was it possible ever to forget?*

He walked down the streets of Moneb, striding as a tall man strides, his head erect, a proud fire in his eyes. The dark-haired folk with skins of golden copper watched him from the doorways and sent the name of Keogh whispering up the lanes and the twisting alleys.

It came to Simon that there was yet another thing in the air of Moneb – a thing called fear.

They came to the gates in the inner wall. Here Harker dropped helplessly back with the other men, and Simon and the son of Keogh went on alone.

Temple and palace rose above him, impressive and strong, bearing in heroic frescoes the history of the kings of Moneb. Simon hardly saw them. There was a tightness in him now, a gathering of nerves.

This was the test – now, before he was ready for it. This was the time when he must not falter, or the thing he had done would be for nothing, and the Harpers would be brought into the valley of Moneb.

Two round towers of brick, a low and massive doorway. Dimness, lighted by torches, red light flaring on coppery flesh, on the ceremonial robes of the councilors, here and there on a helmet of barbaric design. Voices, clamoring over and through each other. A feeling of tension so great that the nerves screamed with it.

Dion pressed his arm and said something that Simon did not catch, but the smile, the look of love and pride, were unmistakable. Then the boy was gone, to the shadowy benches beyond.

Simon stood alone.

At one end of the low, oblong hall, beside the high, gilded seat of the king, he saw a group of helmeted men looking toward him with hatred they did not even try to conceal, and with it, a contempt that could only come from triumph.

And suddenly, from out of the uneasy milling of the throng before him, an old man stepped and put his hands on Simon's shoulders, and peered at him with anguished eyes.

"It is too late, John Keogh," the old man said hoarsely. "It is all for nothing. They have brought the Harpers in!"

IV

THE HARPERS

S imon felt a cold shock of recoil. He had not looked for this. He had not expected that now, this soon, he might be called upon to meet the Harpers.

He had met them once before, years ago. He knew the subtle and terrible danger of them. It had shaken him badly then, when he was a brain divorced from flesh. What would it do to him, now that he dwelt again in a vulnerable, unpredictable human body?

His hand closed tightly on the tiny metal box in his pocket. He must gamble that it would protect him from the Harper's power. But, remembering that experience of years ago, he dreaded the test.

He asked the old councilor, "Do you know this to be true, about the Harpers?"

"Taras and two others were seen at dawn, coming back from the forest, each bearing a hidden thing. And – they wore the Helmets of Silence."

The old man gestured toward the group of men by the king's throne who looked with such triumphant hatred at he whom they thought to be John Keogh.

"See, they wear them still!"

Swiftly, Simon studied the helmets. At first glance, they had seemed no more than the ordinary bronze battle-gear of a barbaric warrior. Now he saw that they were of curious design, covering the ears and the entire cranial area, and overlarge as though padded with many layers of some insulating material.

The Helmets of Silence. He knew, now, that Keogh had spoken truly when he told of an ancient means of protection used long ago by the men of Moneb against the Harpers. Those helmets would protect, yes.

The king of Moneb rose from his throne. And the nervous uproar in the hall stilled to a frozen tension.

A young man, the king. Very young, very frightened, weakness and stubbornness mingled in his face. His head was bare.

"We of Moneb have too long tolerated strangers in our valley – have even suffered one of them to sit in this council and influence our decisions," he began.

Here there was a sharp uneasy turning of heads toward "Keogh."

"The strangers' ways more and more color the lives of our people. They must go – all of them! And since they will not go willingly, they must be forced!"

He had learned the speech by rote. Simon knew that from the way in which he stumbled over it, the way in which his eyes slid to the tallest of the cloaked and helmeted men beside him, for prompting and strength. The dark, tall man whom Simon recognized from Harker's description as Keogh's chief enemy, Taras.

"We cannot force the Earthmen out with our darts and spears. Their weapons are too strong. But we too have a weapon, one they cannot fight! It was forbidden to us, by foolish kings who were afraid it might be used against them. But now we must use it.

"Therefore, I demand that the old tabu be lifted! I demand that we invoke the power of the Harpers to drive the Earthmen forth!"

There was a taut, unhappy silence in the hall. Simon saw men looking at him, the eager confidence in young Dion's eyes. He knew that they placed in him their desperate last hope of preventing this thing.

They were right, for whatever was done he must do alone. Curt Newton and Otho could not possibly have yet made their way secretly by back ways to this council hall.

Simon strode forward. He looked around him. Because of what he was, a kind of fierce exaltation took him, to be once more a man among men. It made his voice ring loud, thundering from the low vault.

"It is not true that the king fears, not the Earthmen, but Taras – and that Taras is bent not on freeing Moneb from a mythical yoke, but in placing one of his own upon our necks?"

There was a moment of utter silence in which they all, king and councilors alike, stared at him aghast. And in the silence, Simon said grimly: "I speak for the council! There will be no lifting of tabu – and he that brings the Harpers into Moneb does so under pain of death!"

For one short moment, the councilors recovered their courage and voiced it. The hall shook with the cheering. Under cover of the noise, Taras bent and spoke into the king's ear, and Simon saw the face of the king become pallid.

From behind the high seat, Taras lifted a helmet embossed in gold and placed it on the king's head. A Helmet of Silence.

The cheering faded, and was not.

The king said hoarsely, "Then for the good of Moneb, I must disband the council."

Taras stepped forward. He looked directly at Simon, and his eyes smiled. "We had foreseen your traitorous counsels, John Keogh. And so we came prepared."

He flung back his cloak. Beneath it, in the curve of his left arm, was something wrapped in silk.

Simon instinctively stepped back.

Taras ripped the silk away. And in his hands was a living creature no larger than a dove, a thing of silver and rose-pearl and delicate frills of shining membrane, and large, soft, gentle eyes.

A dweller in the deep forest, a shy sweet bearer of destruction, an angel of madness and death.

A Harper!

A low moan rose among the councilors, and there was a shifting and a swaying of bodies poised for flight. Taras said, "Be still. There is time enough for running, when I give you leave."

The councilors were still. The king was still, white-faced upon his throne. But on the shadowy benches, Simon saw Keogh's son bend forward, yearning toward the man he thought to be his father, his face alight with a child's faith.

Taras stroked the creature in his hands, his head bent low over it.

The membranous frills began to lift and stir. The rose-pearl body pulsed, and there broke forth a ripple of music like the sound of a muted harp, infinitely sweet and distant.

The eyes of the Harper glowed. It was happy, pleased to be released from the binding silk that had kept its membranes useless for the making of music. Taras continued to stroke it gently, and it responded with a quivering freshet of song, the liquid notes running and trilling upon the silent air.

And two more of the helmeted men brought forth silvery, soft-eyed captives from under their cloaks, and they began to join their music together, timidly at first, and then more and more without hesitation, until the council hall was full of the strange wild harping and men stood still because they were too entranced now to move.

Even Simon was not proof against that infinitely poignant tide of thrilling sound. He felt his body respond, every nerve quivering with a pleasure akin to pain.

He had forgotten the effect of music on the human consciousness. For many years, he had forgotten music. Now, suddenly, all those long-closed gates between mind and body were flung open by the soaring song of the Harpers. Clear, lovely, thoughtless, the very voice of life unfettered, the music filled Simon with an aching hunger for he knew not what. His mind wandered down vague pathways thronged with shadows, and his heart throbbed with a solemn joy that was close to tears.

Caught in the sweet wild web of that harping, he stood motionless, dreaming, forgetful of fear and danger, of everything except that somewhere in that music was the whole secret of creation, and that he was poised on the very edge of understanding the subtle secret of that song.

Song of a newborn universe joyously shouting its birth-cry, of young suns calling to each other in exultant strength, the thunderous chorus of star-voices and the humming bass of the racing, spinning worlds!

Song of life, growing, burgeoning, bursting, on every world, complicated counterpoint of a million million species voicing the ecstasy of being in triumphant chorus!

Something deep in Simon Wright's tranced mind warned him that he was being trapped by that hypnotic web of sound, that he was falling deeper, deeper, into the Harpers' grip. But he could not break the spell of that singing.

Soaring singing of the leaf drinking the sun, of the bird on the wing, of the beast warm in its burrow, of the young, bright miracle of love, of birth, of living!

And then the song changed. The beauty and joy faded from it, and into the sounds came a note of terror, growing, growing…

It came to Simon then that Taras was speaking to the thing he held, and that the soft eyes of the Harper were afraid.

The creature's simple mind was sensitive to telepathic impulses, and Taras was filling its mild emptiness with thoughts of danger and of pain, so that its membranes shrilled now to a different note.

The other Harpers picked it up. Shivering, vibrating together and across each other's rhythms, the three small rose-pearl beings flooded the air with a shuddering sound that was the essence of all fear.

Fear of a blind universe that lent its creatures life only to snatch it from them, of the agony and death that always and forever must rend the bright fabric of the living! Fear of the somber depths of darkness and pain into which all life must finally descend, of the shadows that closed down so fast, so fast!

That awful threnody of primal terror that shuddered from the Harpers struck icy fingers of dread across the heart. Simon recoiled from it, he could not bear it, he knew that if he heard it long ago, he must go mad.

Only dimly was he aware of the terror among the other councilors, the writhing of their faces, the movements of their hands. He tried to cry out but his voice was lost in the screaming of the Harpers, going ever higher and higher until it was torture to the body.

And still Taras bent over the Harper, cruel-eyed, driving it to frenzy with the power of his mind. And still the Harpers screamed, and now the sound had risen and part of it had slipped over the threshold of hearing, and the super-sonic notes stabbed the brain like knives.

A man bolted past Simon. Another followed, and another, and then more and more, clawing, trampling, falling, floundering in the madness of panic. And he himself must flee!

He would **not** flee! Something held him from the flight his body craved – some inner core of thought hardened and strengthened by his long divorcement from the flesh. It steadied him, made him fight back with iron resolution, to reality.

His shaking hand drew out the little metal box. The switch clicked. Slowly, as the power of the thing built up, it threw out a high, shrill keening sound.

"The one weapon against the Harpers!" Curt had said. "The only thing that can break sound is – sound!"

The little repeller reached out its keening sonic vibrations and caught at the Harpers' terrible singing, like a claw.

It clawed and twisted and broke that singing. It broke it, by its subtle sonic interference, into shrieking dissonances.

Simon strode forward, toward the throne and toward Taras. And now into the eyes of Taras had come a deadly doubt.

The Harpers, wild and frightened now, strove against the keening sound that broke their song into hideous discord. The shuddering sonic struggle raged, much of it far above the level of hearing, and Simon felt his body plucked and shaken by terrible vibrations.

He staggered, but he went on. The faces of Taras and the others were contorted by pain. The king had fainted on his throne.

Storm of shattered harmonies, of splintered sound, shrieked like the very voice of madness around the throne. Simon, his mind darkening, knew that he could endure no more…

And suddenly, it was over. Beaten, exhausted, the Harpers stilled the wild vibration of their membranes. Utterly silent, they remained motionless in the hands of their captors, their soft eyes glazed with hopeless terror.

Simon laughed. He swayed a little on his feet and said to Taras, "My weapon is stronger than yours!"

Taras dropped the Harper. It crawled away and hid itself beneath the throne. Taras whispered, "Then we must have it from you, Earthman!"

He sprang toward Simon. On his heels came the others, mad with the bitter fury of defeat when they had been so sure of victory.

Simon snatched the audio-disc and raised it to his lips, pressing its button and crying out the one word, "Hurry!"

He felt that it was too late. But not until now, not until this moment when fear conquered the force of tradition, could Curt and Otho have entered this forbidden place without provoking the very outbreak that must be prevented.

Simon went down beneath his attackers' rush. As he went down, he saw that the councilors who had fled were running back to help him. He heard their voices shouting, and he saw the boy Dion among them.

Something struck cruelly against his head, and there was a crushing weight upon him. Someone screamed, and he caught the bright sharp flash of darts through the torchlight.

He tried to rise, but he could not. He was near unconsciousness, aware only of a confusion of movement and ugly sounds. He smelled blood, and he knew pain.

He must have moved, for he found himself on his hands and knees, looking down into the face of Dion. The shank of a copper dart stood out from the boy's breast, and there was a streak of red across the golden skin. His eyes met Simon's, in a dazed, wondering look. He whispered uncertainly:

"Father!"

He crept into Simon's arms. Simon held him, and Dion murmured once more and then sighed. Simon continued to hold him, though the boy had become very heavy and his eyes looked blankly now into nothingness.

It came to Simon that the hall had grown quiet. A voice spoke to him. He lifted his head and saw Curt standing over him, and Otho, both staring at him anxiously. He could not see them clearly. He said, "The boy thought I was his father. He clung to me and called me Father as he died."

Otho took Dion's body and laid it gently on the stones.

Curt said, "It's all over, Simon. We got here in time, and it's all right."

Simon rose. Taras and his men were dead. Those who had tried to foster hatred were gone, and not ever again would Harpers be brought into Moneb. That was what the pale, shaken councilors around him were telling him.

He could not hear them clearly. Not so clearly, somehow, as the fading whisper of a dying boy.

He turned and walked out of the council hall, onto the steps. It was dark now. There were torches flaring, and the wind blew cold, and he was very tired.

Curt stood beside him. Simon said, "I will go back to the ship."

He saw the question in Curt's eyes, the question that he did not quite dare to ask.

Heartsick, Simon spoke the lines that a Chinese poet had written long ago.

"'Now I know that the ties of flesh and blood only bind us to a load of grief and sorrow."

He shook his head. "I will return to what I was. I could not bear the agony of a second human life – no!"

Curt did not answer. He took Simon's arm and they walked together across the court.

Behind them Otho came, carrying gently three small creatures of silver and rose-pearl, who began now to sound ripples of muted music, faint but hopeful at first, then soaring swiftly to a gladness of prisoners newly freed.

They buried the body of John Keogh in the clearing where he had died, and the boy Dion lay beside him. Over them, Curt and Grag and Otho built a cairn of stones with Harker's help.

From the shadows, Simon Wright watched, a small square shape of metal hovering on silent beams, again a living brain severed forever from human form.

It was done, and they parted from Harker and went down through the great booming lichens toward the ship. Curt and the robot and android paused and looked back at the tall cairn towering lonely against the stars.

But Simon did not look back.

CAPTAIN FUTURE WILL RETURN
IN
THE RETURN OF UL QUORN, BOOK III:
1,500 LIGHT YEARS FROM HOME

Curt Newton has vanished! With his nemesis Ul Quorn at his throat and the *Comet* in the hands of Starry Messenger renegades, Captain Future has plummeted into a wormhole leading to...where?

All that's known about the Deneb system is that it was once the home of an advanced race that explored the galaxy before disappearing for mysterious reasons. But Ul Quorn has gone to considerable effort to go there, and since the Magician of Mars never does anything without purpose, it's up to Curt to discover what it is and stop him. Yet Curt is surrounded by his enemies with no help in sight...or is there?

Action, suspense, and an ancient menace await our hero "1,500 Light Years From Home" in the next installment of a space epic!

About The Author:
Allen Steele

Allen Mulherin Steele, Jr. became a full-time science fiction writer in 1988, following publication of his first short story, "Live From The Mars Hotel" (*Asimov's,* mid-Dec. 1988). Since then, he has become a prolific author of novels, short stories, and essays, with his work translated into more than a dozen languages worldwide.

Allen was born in Nashville, Tennessee. He received his B.A. in Communications from New England College in Henniker, New Hampshire, and his M.A. in Journalism from the University of Missouri in Columbia, Missouri. Before turning to SF, he worked as a staff writer for daily and weekly newspapers in Tennessee, Missouri, and Massachusetts, freelanced for business and general-interest magazines in the Northeast, and spent a short tenure as a Washington correspondent, covering politics on Capitol Hill.

His twenty-one novels include *Orbital Decay*, *Time Loves A Hero* (originally titled *Chronospace)*, *V-S Day*, *Arkwright* and the Coyote series*: Coyote, Coyote Rising, Coyote Frontier, Coyote Horizon* and *Coyote Destiny;* and spin-off novels: *Spindrift, Galaxy Blues, Hex, Apollo's Outcast.* His first Captain Future novel, *Avengers of the Moon,* was published in 2017.

Allen's short fiction has appeared in most major American SF magazines, including *Asimov's Science Fiction, Analog,* and *Fantasy & Science Fiction,* as well as in dozens of anthologies. He has published seven short-fiction collections, including *Rude Astronauts, Sex and Violence in Zero-G: The Complete Near Space Stories,* and *Tales of Time and Space.*

His novella "The Death Of Captain Future" (*Asimov's,* Oct.1995) received the 1996 Hugo Award for Best Novella, won a 1996 *Science Fiction Weekly* Reader Appreciation Award, and received the 1998 Seiun Award for Best Foreign Short Story from Japan's National Science Fiction Convention. It was also a finalist for a 1997 Nebula Award by the Science Fiction and Fantasy Writers of America. Allen's novella "...Where Angels Fear to Tread" (*Asimov's,* Oct./Nov. 1997) received the Hugo Award, the Locus Award, the *Asimov's* Readers Award, and the *Science Fiction Chronicle* Readers Award in 1998, and was a finalist for the Nebula, Sturgeon, and Seiun awards. His novelette, "The Emperor of Mars" (*Asimov's,* June 2010) won the 2011 Hugo Award for Best Novelette and also the *Asimov's* Readers Award.

His novelette "The Good Rat" (*Analog,* mid-Dec. 1995) was a Hugo finalist in 1996, and his novelette "Zwarte Piet's Tale" (*Analog,* Dec. 1998) won an AnLab Award from *Analog* and was a Hugo finalist in 1999. His novelette "Agape Among the Robots" (*Analog,* May 2000) was a finalist for the Hugo in 2001. His novella "Stealing Alabama" (*Asimov's,* January 2001) was a Hugo finalist in 2002 and won the *Asimov's* Readers' Award for that year. His novelette "The Days Between" (*Asimov's* March 2001) was a Hugo finalist in 2002 and a Nebula finalist in 2003. His novella "Liberation Day" and novelette "The Garcia Narrows Bridge" both won the *Asimov's* Readers Awards in 2005. *Orbital Decay* received the 1990 Locus Award for Best First Novel, and *Clarke County, Space* was a finalist for the 1991 Philip K. Dick Award.

Allen was First Runner-Up for the 1990 John W. Campbell Award, received the Donald A. Wollheim Award in 1993, and the Phoenix Award in 2002. In 2013, he received the Robert A. Heinlein Award in recognition of his long career in writing space fiction.

He is a former member of both the Board of Directors and the Board of Advisers for the Science Fiction and Fantasy Writers of America, and is also a former adviser for the Space Frontier Foundation. In April, 2001, he testified before the Subcommittee on Space and Aeronautics of the US House of Representatives in hearings regarding space exploration in the twenty-first century. "Live from the Mars Hotel" is among the many stories and novels included on the "Visions of Mars" disk aboard NASA's Phoenix lander, which landed on Mars in 2008.

Allen lives in western Massachusetts with his wife Linda and their dogs. You can find him on Facebook: www.facebook.com/Allensteelesfwriter .

About the Creator:
Edmond Hamilton

Edmond Hamilton was one of the pioneering authors of American science fiction, and is considered by most genre historians to be one of the fathers of modern space opera.

Born in Youngstown, Ohio in 1904, Hamilton was considered a child prodigy, entering college at age fourteen and graduating just three years later with a degree in electrical engineering. Yet he was more of an imagineer than an inventor, so his lifelong avocation became writing rather than electronics.

Like many imaginative young men and women of his time, Hamilton was drawn to the new genre of "scientifiction." Although his first short story, "The Monster-God of Mamurth," published in the August 1926 issue of *Weird Tales,* was fantasy in the vein of A. Merritt, his second story, "Across Space," later that year in the same magazine began to set the mold for most of the work that would define his literary career for the next fifty years.

In the August 1928 issue of *Weird Tales*, Hamilton published the first installment of a two-part short novel, "Crashing Suns." In the very same month, rival magazine *Amazing Stories,* Edward E. Smith (with collaborator Lee Hawkins Garby) published the first installment of "The Skylark of Space" and Philip Francis Nowlan's cover story "Armageddon 2419 A.D." These three stories, published simultaneously, established a new subgenre of science-fiction adventure that would eventually be labeled "space opera." From the beginning, together with Murray Leinster (Will F. Jenkins) and close friend Jack Williamson, Ed Hamilton would be one of its foremost progenitors, earning him the nickname "World-Wrecker Hamilton" (or alternately "World-Saver Hamilton") among SF fans.

In 1939, Standard Magazines publisher Leo Margulis and editor Mort Weisinger approached Hamilton with the proposal to flesh out a concept they had for a pulp hero they called "Mister Future." Hamilton quickly realized that their character – a wizened dwarf with a giant brain – was too limited to anchor a series, and retooled him and his companions as Captain Future and the Futuremen. The first issue of *Captain Future, Wizard of Science* was published at the end of 1939, and continued quarterly through 1944 when, along with many other pulps, it was killed by the wartime paper shortage.

Although many fans disparaged Captain Future as juvenile, it remains one of the most enduring creations of SF's Golden Age, translated around the world and frequently reprinted to this day. Following his final Captain Future story, "Birthplace of Creation," in the May 1951 issue of *Startling Stories,* Hamilton would continue writing SF for the rest of his life. Hamilton's 1950 novel *The Star Kings* (first published in *Amazing,* September 1947), has seldom been out of print for long, and is regarded today as one of the classics of science fiction; his 1952 short story "What's It Like Out There?" is also considered a classic. He also wrote comic book scripts for DC, including stories for Superman, Batman, and the Legion of Superheroes.

Hamilton was married to fellow author Leigh Brackett. Although they officially collaborated just once, his influence can be felt in his wife's screenplay for the second *Star Wars* movie, *The Empire Strikes Back.* He passed away at his home in California in 1977.

Copyright © 2020 by Coyote Steele LLC

About The Cover Artist:
Renan Boé

Renan Boé is an illustrator, concept artist and graphic designer currently living in São Paulo, Brazil.

Renan graduated from São Paulo State University (UNESP) in graphic design. While there, he always looked for people who had the same desire to pursue a career as an illustrator in order to share their experience. He learned a lot that way.

Since childhood, Renan has had an interest in working in the entertainment industry as a digital artist; he practiced drawing and painting from then. He has always been fascinated by works of fiction and fantasy, themes that he has specialized in in recent years.

Renan's works can be found on ArtStation (https://www.artstation.com/renanboe) and Instagram (https://www.instagram.com/renan.boe).

About The Interior Artist:
M. D. Jackson

M.D. Jackson has been drawing since he was old enough to hold a pencil. He has been a professional artist, designer and illustrator for over 30 years. His work has appeared in numerous magazines and on countless book covers.

M.D. Works mostly in a digital medium (because it is the 21st century), but happily is also handy with an ink pen and, of course, that old tested and true technology of the HB pencil and a scrap of paper.

About the Comet II Artist:
Rob Caswell

With a formal education in electro-mechanical drawing and astrophysics, Rob Caswell's scientific and science fiction illustration is the closest he gets these days to professionally applying his academic training. Rob has been a space hardware and cosmic adventure junkie since growing up in New Hampshire during the 60s space race, where he developed on a diet of *Space Angel* cartoons and Gerry Anderson TV shows.

Rob began his professional scifi illustration career in the eighties, primarily through paper-and-pen role-playing games (RPGs) such as *Traveller, Star Wars, Paranoia, 2300 A.D,, Space: 1889,* et al. He's also worked as a draftsman, comic book letterer, RPG editor and writer, computer game designer and artist, web designer, photo retoucher, digital printer, and illustrator for science fiction books. His artwork inspired the *Star Trek: Seekers* novel series by Simon & Schuster, for which he ultimately provided the cover art.

Meeting in the late 90s, Rob and Allen Steele formed a fast friendship over their numerous shared passions, dominated by science fiction and scale modeling. Rob has worked as an illustrator and designer of cover and interior technical illustrations on a number of Allen's projects, starting with the 2008 novel *Galaxy Blues.*

Rob crafted the design of the original Captain Future *Comet* which appeared inside *Avengers of the Moon.* Charged with the job of bringing the *Comet II* to life – Captain Future's succeeding set of cosmic wheels after the first ship's demise – Rob tried to both channel the Space-X and Scaled Composites inspired design ethos he'd applied to the original while taking it in a newer, grander direction. The result was a ship that dictated its own form from the loose details as it evolved in discussions and in the sketchbook, surprising both Rob and Allen with its final configuration.

Rob lives in Western Massachusetts in the foothills of the Berkshires, with is wife Deb Zeigler and a diverse variety of "wild guest/pets" buzzing, chirping, digging, grazing, and just passing through their woody yard. He currently operates Evolv Fine Art Printing – a giclée print studio in Easthampton, MA. You can see more of his art at: www.deviantart.com/rob-caswell.

Made in the USA
San Bernardino, CA
08 June 2020

72945444R00115